She had amnesia. And the doctor was saying she was pregnant.

Her name was Jenny Prentice. She repeated it silently, slowly. A man named Luke claimed she was his wife. And she had a baby growing inside her. The weight of all this staggering news had her reeling.

Baby. Instinctively, she smoothed a protective hand over her abdomen.

"Jenny," Luke said, disbelief in his eyes, "why didn't you tell me?"

All she could do was look at him helplessly. She couldn't help but wonder what kind of woman would keep such wonderful news from her husband.

"I might be able to shed some light on this situation."

All eyes turned to Luke's brother, Chad, as they waited for him to explain himself.

"I'm sorry you have to find out like this, Luke," Chad continued. "But I think Jenny didn't tell anyone about the baby because…well, to put it bluntly, I think I may be the baby's father."

Dear Reader,

Traditionally June is the month for weddings, so Silhouette Romance cordially invites you to enjoy our promotion JUNE BRIDES, starting with Suzanne Carey's *Sweet Bride of Revenge*. In this sensuously powerful VIRGIN BRIDES tale, a man forces the daughter of his nemesis to marry him, never counting on falling in love with the enemy....

Up-and-comer Robin Nicholas delivers a touching BUNDLES OF JOY titled *Man, Wife and Little Wonder*. Can a denim-clad, Harley-riding bad boy turn doting dad and dedicated husband? Find out in this classic marriage-of-convenience romance! Next, Donna Clayton's delightful duo MOTHER & CHILD continues with the evocative title *Who's the Father of Jenny's Baby?* A woman awakens in the hospital to discover she has amnesia—and she's pregnant! Problem is, *two* men claim to be the baby's father—her estranged husband...and her husband's brother!

Granted: Wild West Bride is the next installment in Carol Grace's BEST-KEPT WISHES series. This richly Western romance pairs a toughened, taut-muscled cowboy and a sophisticated city gal who welcomes his kisses, but will she accept his ring? For a fresh spin on the bridal theme, try Alice Sharpe's *Wife on His Doorstep*. An about-to-be bride stops her wedding to the wrong man, only to land on the doorstep of the strong, silent ship captain who was to perform the ill-fated nuptials.... And in Leanna Wilson's latest Romance, *His Tomboy Bride*, Nick Latham was *supposed* to "give away" childhood friend and bride-to-be Billie Rae—not claim the transformed beauty as his own!

We hope you enjoy the month's wedding fun, and return each and every month for more classic, emotional, heartwarming novels from Silhouette Romance.

Enjoy!

Joan Marlow Golan

Joan Marlow Golan
Senior Editor Silhouette Romance

Please address questions and book requests to:
Silhouette Reader Service
U.S.: 3010 Walden Ave., P.O. Box 1325, Buffalo, NY 14269
Canadian: P.O. Box 609, Fort Erie, Ont. L2A 5X3

WHO'S THE FATHER OF JENNY'S BABY?

Donna Clayton

Silhouette

R O M A N C E™

Published by Silhouette Books

America's Publisher of Contemporary Romance

For Dorothy B. Montgomery
My Aunt Dot
With Love

SILHOUETTE BOOKS

ISBN 0-373-19302-5

WHO'S THE FATHER OF JENNY'S BABY?

Copyright © 1998 by Donna Fasano

This edition published by arrangement with Harlequin Books S.A.

® and TM are trademarks of Harlequin Books S.A., used under license.
Trademarks indicated with ® are registered in the United States Patent
and Trademark Office, the Canadian Trade Marks Office and in other
countries.

Printed in U.S.A.

DONNA CLAYTON

is proud to be a recipient of the Holt Medallion, an award honoring outstanding literary talent. And seeing her work appear on the Waldenbooks Series bestsellers list has given her a great deal of joy and satisfaction.

Reading is one of Donna's favorite ways to while away a rainy afternoon. She loves to hike, too. Another hobby added to her list of fun things to do is traveling. She fell in love with Europe during her first trip abroad recently and plans to return often. Oh, and Donna still collects cookbooks, but as her writing career grows, she finds herself using them less and less.

Mother & Child

Thoughts On Motherhood
by Jenny Prentice

The doctor tells me I'm carrying a child. Even with no memory of the past and no idea who fathered this baby, the very idea that I'm pregnant fills me with awe and wonder. Babies conjure up images of soft, rosy skin and trusting eyes. I can easily imagine holding my infant to my breast, smelling the powdery scent of his tiny body close to mine, counting his fingers and toes, singing sweet lullabies until he falls gently to sleep, tucking him in with a satiny blanket, kissing his chubby cheek. When the reality of my situation becomes overwhelming, I escape into thoughts such as these.

I don't know what kind of woman I might have been to have allowed two men to claim the baby growing inside me. I have no clue who is telling the truth. Who is the one I should listen to. Who is the one I can trust.

But when I think of my baby, all those uncertainties seem to fade away into nothing. All that matters is that my child enter this world knowing he is loved, knowing he is cared for, knowing he is wanted. Who I was, who I might have been, matters little. Who I am and who I will be is all-important.

I want only the very best for my child.

Chapter One

She came awake slowly, as if she'd been ensnared for an eternity in the deepest of sleeps. The warm fuzziness threatened to pull her back into the protective depths of slumber; however, the flurry of activity she sensed taking place around her was too disturbing, too confusing, and she was forced to shrug off the dreamy hands tugging at her, enticing her back into oblivion.

With great effort, she raised her eyelids and was immediately blinded by the powerful light shining down from directly overhead. A small unbidden moan passed her lips. Turning her head away from the bright light, she immediately regretted the movement as a giant wave of nausea washed over her. She squeezed her eyes shut and tried not to move.

"She's coming to. Get the doctor in here. Now."

The man's voice sounded unfamiliar to her, but the intense, barely suppressed emotion lacing the rich resonance of his words sent a shiver coursing down her spine. She couldn't help but wonder who he was.

The query, innocently whispered through the foggy haze in her brain, seemed to pry open a floodgate through which other questions tumbled and churned, one on top of the other.

Where was she? What was happening? What had brought her to this place? Why was every muscle in her body throbbing like an abscessed tooth? And why didn't someone turn off that glaring light?

"Jenny? Come on, now, wake up."

A different voice, her mind deciphered. Male, also. But softer than the first. Less angry. However, this one, too, was tinged with emotion. The edginess pervading the second man's words nearly made her skin crawl, and for the first time since awakening, she felt fear.

It was purely her survival instinct that had her forcing her eyes open once again. If danger was coming, she wanted to see its approach.

What a strange idea to enter her head, she thought, lifting her hand to shield her gaze from the bright light. The dark sensation that she was somehow in jeopardy dissolved, like valley mist burned off by the rising sun, as she focused all her energy on making out the gray shapes moving beyond the light.

"Can't you see she's being blinded?"

She knew it was the first man, the angry one, who batted the overhead light fixture aside so it no longer shone directly into her face. Her senses were momentarily overloaded as she tried to take in everything at once.

White. Everything was white. The walls, the bed linens, the uniformed-clad nurses...

A hospital. She was in the—

"Hospital."

The murmured word, rusty and trembling, came from her lips, but the sound of it was so strange. As if she was hearing it for the very first time. This was bizarre. Why wouldn't she recognize the sound of her own voice?

Seeds of panic and confusion sprouted in her chest, her heart pounding against her ribs in unison with the pain pounding in her head. She pressed her fingertips to her lips. In an effort to curb the rush of anxiety flooding through her, she forced her eyes to focus on the first object on which they landed.

A face.

The man stood at the foot of the bed, directly in front of her. He was dark, tawny, a man who most assuredly worked outside in the sun. He was handsome, in spite of the tension tightening his hawklike features. The artificial light glistened on his raven hair, and his coal-black eyes were etched with intensity—an intensity that told her, in no uncertain terms, that this was the owner of the first voice she'd heard upon awakening.

"There was an accident," he told her. "You took a tumble."

"Ha! Luke, only you would describe what happened to Jenny as a *tumble*."

She allowed her gaze to leave the dark, angry man's face, but not before noting his name.

The man who addressed Luke was standing at her bedside. His was the voice that had induced in her that odd feeling of peril only moments ago, but as she looked at him, she couldn't help but wonder why she would have had that reaction. He certainly didn't seem like a person who would invoke fear in anyone.

His sandy hair looked tousled, and a cheery smile lit his brown eyes as he turned his gaze on her. "You slid about two hundred feet down the mountainside, Jenny," he said. "We didn't find you for hours. You had us all scared to death."

There it was again, she noted. That nervous, jittery quality in his voice. Why should that frighten her so?

Without warning, a renewed panic blossomed inside her, shooting forth like a wild, fast-growing vine. The trepidation curling in her belly was hot and terrifying. Her eyes widened with this seemingly irrational dread, and for some odd reason, her gaze fled to the face of the dark, angry man—Luke, she remembered—for some sort of comfort, or protection, or something, even though it made no sense to her why she would feel afraid *or* why she would seek help from this complete stranger.

Evidently, the man named Luke noticed her emotional state because he tossed an irritated glare at the sandy-haired man.

"Shut up, Chad," he said.

But Chad didn't shut up. In fact, his nervousness seemed to increase until it no longer showed just in his voice, but in his eyes, too.

"You'll be fine, now," Chad went on. "You'll come home, and everything will be just fine. Won't it, Jenny?"

She opened her mouth to speak, to ask one of the dozens of questions buzzing like so many bees in her throbbing head, but before she could, Chad snatched up a cup that had been sitting on the bedside table.

"Would you like a drink of water, Jenny?" He offered her the cup.

The confusion swimming in her brain was more than she could bear. Pressing her palms to her temples, she ignored the painful protest of her aching body as she inched away from both men to the far corner of the bed.

"Why do you keep calling me that?"

The question burst from her in a fit of near hysteria, making her head thud all the more. She was vaguely aware that the one nurse who had been in the examination room had slipped silently out the door.

"Calling you what?" Chad said, seeming totally surprised by her outburst. "Jenny? Why, it's your name, of course. What's wrong with you, silly?" He then tossed her a knowing look, as though he were on to her. "All right now, this is no time for pranks."

His thin, jittery chuckle seemed to smack her across the face. Didn't he see the turmoil she was experiencing? Couldn't he understand that her whole world had turned upside down?

"Would you shut up, Chad!"

Luke's sharp order made the younger man go silent, but it only succeeded in frightening her more than ever. She felt like a small, helpless animal, cornered, with nowhere to run.

"Now, listen to me…"

Her attention was drawn by Luke's calm, commanding tone. Through the drumming agony in her head, she noticed that the anger in his black eyes had been replaced with what looked like deep concern as he gently coaxed her with his soft words.

"The nurse has gone for the doctor."

He placed his hand on her shin. The thin cotton blanket between her skin and his was inadequate protection against his burning touch. She was unable to keep the panic from her eyes, her gaze darting to his fingertips, and it took every ounce of her control to hold back the whimper threatening to escape from her throat. He immediately removed his hand from her leg.

"I'm Luke," he continued smoothly, quietly. "Luke Prentice. Your husband. And this is my brother, Chad."

Her *husband?* Had he really said that? Why didn't she know him? She didn't remember being part of a wedding.

She didn't remember having a honeymoon. She would never forget the happiness of a wedding day! This was some sort of cruel joke. Her eyes welled with tears of confusion and her hands trembled violently.

"This is crazy, Luke." Chad ran his fingers through his disheveled hair. "She knows who we are—"

"Would you look at her?" Luke's chin snapped up as he frowned at his brother. "She's scared witless. She doesn't even know her own name. She's looking at us like we're total strangers."

He inhaled deeply as he studied her face, evidently forcing himself to calm down.

"It's okay, Jenny," he told her, his face filled with concern. "The doctor's on his way. He'll help you. You're going to be okay."

She felt he was chanting the positive affirmation for his own benefit almost as much as for her. Even though her entire existence had suddenly turned to utter chaos, she still had enough of her wits about her to realize that he, too, was experiencing a shock. And for one quick moment, her heart went out to him as well as to the other man, the sandy-haired man. Chad was his name, she reminded herself.

Then Chad said, "Of course she's going to be okay."

The tone of his voice changed to such a degree that she was astounded. The flustered quality that she'd found so frightening disappeared so swiftly, so thoroughly, that she was left wondering if she hadn't imagined it from the beginning. Or was it that the flash of sympathy she felt for him had made her lower her guard?

Was the fear she had felt illogical? she wondered. Darting a fleeting look at his face, she again saw nothing frightening in Chad's friendly smile. She crossed her arms, hugging herself tightly, and let her gaze light momentarily on Luke. What made her think she was any less vulnerable to this onyx-eyed man?

Her head whirled with pain and bewilderment. Smoothing her fingertips across her forehead, she murmured, "My head hurts."

"Where the hell is the doctor?" Luke turned and took a step toward the door.

"He's coming," Chad assured them both.

An elderly man came into the room, his lab coat pristine white but terribly rumpled.

"It's about time," Luke growled at him.

"Hey, Doc Porter," Chad greeted him breezily.

The doctor ignored both men and moved directly to her side.

"Well, Jenny Prentice," he said, "the nurse tells me you're having a little trouble with your memory. Seems you might be suffering from a touch of amnesia."

A touch of amnesia? If her head hadn't been thumping like the devil was dancing a drunken jig on her brain, she'd have laughed right out loud, despite the jumbled state of her memory.

"Let's have a look at you." The doctor took a small penlight from the pocket of his coat and proceeded to shine it first in her right eye and then in her left. "Good pupil reflex," he said. Tucking the pen away, he leaned back and looked into her face. "So what can you tell me about yourself, Jenny Prentice?" he asked.

She got the distinct impression that he'd stated her full name twice in order to get her used to the sound of it. But everything around her seemed so foreign, so unfamiliar, that she simply remained mute.

"Can you tell me how old you are?" he asked.

She shook her head.

"The name of our town?"

Again she shook her head.

"What state do you live in?"

This time she didn't bother to answer. She just drew her bottom lip between her teeth in an effort to keep her tears at bay. How could her memory be so...empty?

"How about these rascals here in the room with us?" With a small jerk of his head, the doctor indicated the two men standing at her bedside. "Do you recognize them?"

Her breathing grew shallow, and she felt sure she would lose all control. Using every ounce of determination she could muster, she forced back the anxiety.

"I know their names are Luke and Chad," she said slowly, her voice a grating whisper. "And Luke told me—" Her breath caught in her throat. She took a moment to steel herself, then began again. "He said he was my husband."

"Well," Doc Porter said, patting her shoulder in gentle consolation, "that's a start." He turned his attention to Luke. "I want to keep Jenny overnight. I want to keep an eye on her." His face wrinkled with a smile. "I'm happy to report some good news. The X-rays show no sign of concussion, and the fall she took doesn't seem to have hurt the baby."

The room grew utterly still and quiet.

"The *what?*" Luke's features had gone lax with pure, unadulterated astonishment.

She sat motionless. The doctor was saying she was pregnant. This was all just too much to take in.

Her name was Jenny Prentice. She repeated it silently, slowly. She was married. And she had a baby growing inside her. The weight of all this staggering news had her reeling. It was a wonder she didn't faint dead away. But she didn't.

Maybe it was a strong sense of survival, maybe it was

a deep, innate maternal instinct, but whatever the cause, she found herself zeroing in on one single word.

Baby. Instinctively, she smoothed a protective hand over her lower abdomen. She was going to have a baby.

"My God, Jenny," Luke said, disappointment in her showing plainly in his eyes, "why didn't you tell me?"

All she could do was look at him helplessly. This was all news to her, too. But as she looked at his devastated expression, she couldn't help but wonder what kind of woman would keep such wonderful news from her husband?

"Maybe I didn't know." Her tone was weak, even to her own ears, and she looked at the doctor, hoping for a confirmation.

The old man shook his head. "You came to my office for the test two weeks ago, Jenny. You've had the results for a while."

"I don't understand," Luke said.

His midnight gaze threatened to bore a hole right through her. But she couldn't help him, because she didn't understand any of this, either. She could give him no answers, offer him no solace, not when she was so overwhelmed by the total blank that was her memory.

"I might be able to shed some light on this situation."

Every eye in the room was on Chad, and they all waited, seemingly breathless, for him to explain himself.

"I'm sorry you have to find out like this, Luke," Chad continued. "But I think that Jenny didn't tell anyone about the baby because…" He stuffed his hands into the pockets of his tan shorts, heaving a sigh before continuing. "Well, to put it bluntly, I think I may be the baby's father."

Jenny Prentice slipped into the pair of well-worn jeans. She'd have sworn on a stack of Bibles that she'd never laid eyes on them before, yet as she fastened the metal stud and zipped the zipper, she couldn't deny the fact that the soft blue denim fabric fit her body to a T.

Everything felt so strange. Every action seemed new and never-before-performed. Her whole world was an alien place.

Yet, she knew what blue jeans were when the nurse's assistant brought them to her, telling her the clothes had been left for her by her husband. She'd known what the toothbrush was used for. And the brush and comb. However, even though she'd been told these items belonged to her, she'd felt as if she'd been seeing them, using them, for the very first time.

Her overnight stay at the hospital had turned into four days. After the horrible scene that had taken place between the Prentice brothers the day she had awakened after the accident, Jenny had begged Doc Porter to give her some time. Alone. And thankfully, the elderly doctor had complied.

The truth was, she'd been frightened witless by the argument Luke and Chad had had after her pregnancy had been made known. Not that the men had come to blows. Doc had made himself a physical shield between the brothers before that could happen. But the anger and hurt and accusations that had flown back and forth between them had painted a terrible picture in her mind.

What kind of woman would have an affair with her husband's brother right under—

Don't think about this, she urgently ordered herself. But the trouble was, there was nothing else in her brain on which to focus her thoughts. Her memory was simply…gone. So her mind kept coming back to the hideous insinuations made by the brothers. But she just couldn't make herself face the situation, so she'd used that same silent order over and over during these long, lazy days. *Don't think about it.*

Every day, Doc came to visit her. He checked her scratches, her bumps and bruises. Then, every day, he'd ask her if she had any questions about herself, her life, her existence before the accident. And every day she'd answered firmly, negatively.

Jenny wasn't ready. She didn't want to know who she was, what she'd done, who she'd hurt. The implications she'd gathered from the fight the brothers had had were enough to make her terribly afraid of learning the truth. No, nothing was said outright, but the fact that Chad had declared that he was her baby's father had been more than enough.

Realizing she'd once again become lost in dark dread, that she hadn't yet finished dressing, she reached into the bag that contained her clothes. The white, sleeveless top she tugged over her head smelled faintly of honeysuckle. Tucking the hem into the waistband of her jeans, she was extremely aware of the soft fragrance wafting around her.

Was this delicate, flowery perfume what she normally dabbed on her wrists and behind her ears? Was it a fragrance that Luke found alluring?

The unbidden question startled her. She shouldn't be concerning herself with what Luke Prentice might or might not find desirable. Not with so many unanswered questions bombarding her every second since she'd awakened into this new, unknown existence. Like an unconscious sleepwalker, she found herself moving toward the large window, staring out at the view.

Her gaze traveled to the farthest point on the horizon. The mountains in the distance were covered with a thick layer of dense, green trees. She didn't know the name of those mountains. Hadn't even allowed herself to ask Doc or the nurses that simple question, let alone any of the others that plagued her constantly. All she did know was that the mountains calmed her, and she'd spent hours standing here, thinking of nothing, taking solace in the sight.

Staring off at the horizon, she hugged herself and waited for that comfortable, serene feeling to overtake her. But her racing thoughts refused to be arrested, despite the lush green of the mountains. How could she have thought they would, she wondered, when she'd been told just this morning that she would no longer be allowed to take refuge here?

Jenny pressed the flat of her hand against her stomach to quell the rising panic as she pictured in her mind's eye Doc Porter's gaze as he'd accused her, in his gentle, fatherly manner, of using the hospital as a hideout. She hadn't been able to refute Doc's accusation.

Doc had gone on to recommend firmly that she return to Prentice Mountain, saying that the once familiar surroundings of the ski resort might help to jog her memory. Of course, he hadn't been able to promise anything with regard to her amnesia. Brain injuries, he'd explained, were peculiar things that continued to stump modern medicine.

So, Jenny Prentice—as she'd learned to call herself over the past few days—was forced to realize that she might never recover from her amnesia. However, she did have to admit that Doc's parting statement had intrigued her.

"You were never one to hide your head under the covers, Jenny," he'd commented. Then he'd left her alone, intent on finishing his hospital rounds before going to his office to begin his full schedule of patient appointments.

Doc had told her, in no uncertain terms, that the old Jenny was no coward. And as she stood gazing out the window, she knew she liked the idea that she was strong. However, the thought wasn't enough to spur her into any kind of rush to find out more about herself. What might she discover? That she was an adulterer? A betrayer of trust? Someone who lied to and deceived the man with whom she'd chosen to spend the rest of her life?

The questions were daunting. Almost as daunting as the painful expression Luke had leveled at her during their last meeting. Never in a hundred million years would Jenny forget the hurt reflected in her husband's black, staring gaze as Doc had ushered both of the brothers from her room.

She hadn't seen either of the Prentice men since then, at her own request. But that request was no longer being honored. She was being forced to face herself, her life and her past behavior. It didn't matter that she remembered none of these things. There were still deeds that someone needed to be held accountable for.

For the thousandth time in the past four days, her baby came into her thoughts. Her stomach felt flat and firm as she slid her hand across it. Who had fathered the delicate life growing inside her? The question prompted the vivid image of Luke, and his tormented gaze.

His agonized expression had been clear evidence that he'd never even suspected that his wife and his brother might have slept together, let alone the fact that Chad would claim to be her baby's father. Her eyelids closed as she ran headfirst into a solid wall of guilt. What kind of woman would do such a thing? What kind of woman *could* do such a thing?

Don't think about it, she silently ordered herself.

If there was one thing she was sure of, it was that Luke

wouldn't be the one who came to pick her up. It would be a wonder if the man ever spoke to her again.

"Jenny."

She recognized the sound of Luke's voice, its rich resonance causing her eyes to fly open with surprise as she turned to face him.

Well, he was here, she thought. Surprise number one.

Then she noticed something else. He didn't look angry. Or hurt. In fact, Jenny didn't think anyone would ever be able to tell that, just four short days ago, he'd been totally humiliated by her. Surprise number two.

Surprise number three came when he actually smiled at her. It was small, as smiles went, but at the same time it was staggering. Way down deep inside, she felt a spark strike to life.

When she noticed that he was staring at her feet, she asked, "What is it?"

His dark eyes found hers. "Doc said that bump you took on the head might have taken away the old Jenny for good. But she's not far off."

Jenny was surprised by the hope that spurted up inside her. But there was an undeniable dread there, too. Unable to stop herself, she softly asked, "What makes you say that?"

"Your bare feet."

His smile widened into an all-out grin, and the spark grew hotter, licking and dancing deep within her.

"I never could get you to wear shoes," he explained further. "Especially in summer."

Identifying the pure, unadulterated physical attraction for what it was, Jenny was stunned silent. How could this be happening? Why would she feel such a strong pull to Luke when she was supposed to be having an affair with his brother?

The implications made her face flame, made her avert her eyes from his.

Did the old Jenny Prentice have such loose morals that she could sleep with two men? Her insides churned with disgust. What kind of woman was she? she wondered yet again.

"Come on, Jenny," Luke said.

The tightness in his voice told her he'd noticed her embarrassment. She cast him a furtive glance. Sure enough, his smile had disappeared, and his eyes were cool chips of shiny coal.

"Put your shoes on." He moved to the bed and picked up the small bag that contained her meager personal belongings. Turning his back on her, he said, "Let's go home."

She had no choice but to follow him.

Chapter Two

Home. The word should conjure up feelings of security and warmth, happiness and laughter. Togetherness. Sharing. Family. But Jenny felt none of these things. Dread sat in her stomach, heavy as a concrete block, as she contemplated going to a place she didn't remember, living with a man who was a stranger to her.

When she exited the hospital, sunshine warmed her cheeks and she paused long enough to close her eyes for an instant and lift her face skyward. She'd only had a scant moment to enjoy the warm, sunny day before Luke urged her forward, settling his palm on the small of her back.

It was an innocent movement, she was sure. One he'd probably made hundreds of times as her husband, but the jolt that ricocheted up her spine at his touch made her eyes go wide and her knees turn weak.

"We've got a thirty-minute drive ahead of us," he told her, directing her further into the parking lot.

She was relieved that she was able to keep putting one

foot in front of the other in a normal stride. The heat of his hand against her back seemed hotter than the summer sun, scalding her, yet she didn't find it uncomfortable. To the contrary, she found his touch strangely pleasing in a purely physical sense. Before she even realized it, warm tendrils curled down deep in her belly. The low curve of her back seemed like such an unlikely spot for an erogenous zone to be located.

She quickened her pace, hoping to get a step or two ahead of him, and the feel of his hand against her. The last thing she wanted was to let this stranger, no matter how good-looking he might be, see her react to him in such a blatantly physical manner. He might be her husband, but she didn't know this man.

With just a few quick steps, she was able to put some space between them.

"Whoa," he called out.

She stopped and turned to face him.

"You walked right past our Bronco."

Her cheeks were warm and rosy, a leftover reaction to his touch, she knew. His brow wrinkled with a frown as he noticed, and that mortified her.

"It's okay," he assured her. "How could you know?"

She let the tiny, self-conscious smile tug at one corner of her mouth. However, she couldn't help but feel a twinge of guilt because she allowed him to believe her embarrassment was caused by having missed the car and not by the fact that her insides had nearly been melted by the mere touch of his hand. She was just relieved that her response had been, for the most part, internal, and all that had surfaced to draw his attention had been a little heated color on her face.

Luke held open the passenger door of the big, four-wheel-drive vehicle, and Jenny had to use the running board to step up into the cab. He went around to the other side and slid behind the wheel.

"It's so strange," she said, latching the seat belt securely around her waist. "I remember I need to wear a seat belt...but I haven't the slightest idea what town I'm in." She straightened. "I know that that's a rosebush, and that's a pine tree, but I can't remember the name of that mountain range." She pointed toward the horizon.

Turning the key in the ignition, Luke looked her way. "Doc didn't offer to fill you in on that kind of stuff?"

She looked contrite. "Oh, he offered," she said softly. "He made himself available every morning for any questions I might have." Her gaze wandered out the window and her tone dropped to a whisper as she went on. "I was too afraid to ask."

The Bronco sat motionless, the engine idling smoothly.

After a silent moment, Luke softly commented, "That sure doesn't sound like the Jenny I know."

Frustration reared up inside her. First Doc Porter had chastised her, telling her she hadn't been the kind of person to hide from the truth. And now Luke was rebuking her, too. Something in her snapped.

"Don't you understand?" she cried, her eyes welling with tears of defeat and confusion. "The woman you know isn't in here." She tapped her index finger twice against her temple. "I don't remember her. I don't know her. I'm not sure I even want to—"

"Jenny, stop." He reached out toward her, his strong fingers gently encircling her wrist.

"Don't," she whispered pleadingly, and pulled her arm from his grasp. His touch did things to her. Made her feel a hunger that was both confusing and exciting.

Why was that? The question slipped into her consciousness before she could stop it. Why did she react so strongly to him when—

Jenny shoved the thought aside. She wasn't ready. There were simply too many other, more fundamental, questions that needed answers. Questions like—who was Jenny Prentice? And is that woman ever coming back? And what was everyone going to do if she didn't? Who was this man sitting next to her? What kind of marriage had they shared?

That thought brought another startling question. What was he going to expect of her as his wife?

I can't have sex with a total stranger. A flash of panic swept through her.

The idea of sex brought another question rolling into her mind. Who had fathered the baby she carried?

At the thought of the child growing inside her, she settled her hands, one overtop the other, low on her belly. To Jenny, that last question was the most important of all.

Suddenly, honest emotion flooded from her. "I don't understand why you're even here," she told him. "You should have sent someone after me. After what I've done to you. To our marriage." She shook her head. "I don't remember what we had together. I don't have one single memory of our life. But it's got to hurt you to think I might have slept with your brother."

She clamped her lips shut. It hadn't been her intention to reveal so much of the self-doubt she was feeling. Not in such an in-your-face manner, anyway. She had no idea how he might react to such candor.

Her chest seized with guilt as she saw his dark gaze cloud over with pain.

"Look," he said, "first of all, I want you to know that I don't believe you and Chad had an affair. *I'm* the father of the baby you're carrying. I said it four days ago when you first woke up from your fall, and I'm saying it now."

Yes, he was making the declaration. Jenny heard it plain and clear. But there was doubt in his onyx eyes—doubt she couldn't pretend she hadn't noticed.

"But why would Chad—"

He silenced her with an uplifted hand and a slow shake of his head. "There's plenty of time to work it all out," he told her. "You're still battered and bruised. You need to take time to heal." He put the Bronco into reverse and pulled slowly from the parking spot. "We'll find answers to the complicated questions later. For now, let's stick with the simple things."

"Simple things?" she asked, wondering if there really was anything simple in this frighteningly complicated situation.

"Yeah." He nodded, driving to the parking-lot exit and then onto the road. "You can't get much more simple than where we are. So that's where we'll start. We're in Olem, Pennsylvania. On North Street, to be exact. And that mountain range you were asking about? Those are the Pocono Mountains." He reached toward the windshield, pointing to the northwest. "See that one? The one with the jagged top? That's Prentice Mountain. It's where we're heading. That's where we live."

For nearly half an hour, Luke drove the curving back roads, taking every opportunity to point out to her all the interesting spots and the people on the outskirts of the town.

Olem was a small community in the summer, he'd told her. However, the ski season brought home the winter residents who loved the sport, and the already booming tourist industry was growing even more with each passing year.

He pointed out two other resorts along the road weaving toward Prentice Mountain. Jenny noticed that Luke didn't seem threatened by the neighboring businesses, despite the fact that these other resorts must compete for his customers. The way he talked about the other owners, people who should have been his competition, as if they were his friends, made her feel light, almost buoyant. And for the first time all morning, she felt a small smile playing on her lips. Jenny didn't understand what she was feeling, or why she was feeling it. That really didn't matter, she decided, relaxing in her seat to enjoy the rest of this mini tour.

Jenny found herself enjoying the rich rhythm of Luke's voice. His tone sounded mellow and serene, so very different from the angry one she remembered hearing four days earlier in the emergency room.

That was it, she realized. The fact that the harshness had disappeared from his voice had lulled her into this wonderful state of light and easy calm. Luke seemed like a completely different person now than he had four days ago.

She felt the desire to ponder this a little further, but Luke pulled off the road in front of a small farmhouse.

"Bud and Mary live here," Luke told her. "You and I both are addicted to the fresh tomatoes Bud sells. I thought I'd buy us a few. For dinner."

He opened his door, and instinctively, Jenny reached to open hers.

"Sit still," he told her. "The stand's right over there." He pointed. "I'll only be a minute."

Luke went to the produce stand and Jenny heard the friendly murmur of his voice as he greeted the farmer. As if she'd heard the Bronco arrive, a woman came out of the house, wiping her hands on her apron.

"Hi, Jenny," the woman called out across the yard to her, waving. "Glad to see you're okay."

Jenny's body flushed with a wave of anxiety. She was supposed to know this lady. Tentatively, Jenny raised her hand in greeting and tried to smile.

The woman walked across the yard to the produce stand, joining Luke and Bud in conversation. Jenny frowned. It was so obvious from the pitying glances the woman kept tossing toward the Bronco that the three of them were talking about her, and that made her feel self-conscious. Like an outsider.

Didn't they realize that *they* were the strangers? Not her.

She closed her eyes and sighed shakily. Who was she kidding? she silently asked herself. *She* was the one who had changed.

Luke pulled open the door and slipped in beside her, startling her.

"Mary's going to bake us a lemon meringue pie," he said, tucking a brown paper bag filled with ripe, red tomatoes in the space between the front seats. "It's your favorite," he went on.

She darted a quick, covert look at the couple as Luke pulled away. "What did you say to them?" she blurted, unable to hide the defensiveness she felt. "They were looking at me like I have some kind of, of terminal disease."

"That's silly, Jenny," he said, gently. "Of course, they weren't—"

"I'm *not* being silly!"

His jaw tensed with what she took to be irritation. Well, he'd just have to suffer through it, darn it. A little annoyance was nothing compared to the sheer torment she ran headlong into around every corner she turned.

"Look," he said, keeping his eyes on the road ahead, "Bud and Mary are our neighbors. Our friends. They're *your* friends, Jenny. They care about you. I had to tell them something."

"So what did you say?" she rushed to asked. Not giving him an instant to respond, she went on. "'Poor, poor Jenny. She bumped her head and poof—'" she snapped her fingers in the air "'—life as she remembers it just disappeared.'"

She felt herself losing control. Heard the high-pitched quality of her voice as her tongue rushed ahead of logical thought. But like a fast and dangerous avalanche, her emotions seemed to take hold of her and send her, bumping and scraping, over a steep and all-consuming cliff of pure panic.

"I didn't say anything like that," he told her. "But, Jenny, I had to tell them about the amnesia. I had to."

"They think I'm a freak," she cried. "'Take pity on the poor little idiot.'"

Jenny knew what she was saying was nonsensical. She could hear the ridiculousness of what was bubbling up from inside her. Still she was totally helpless to stop it.

"It's not like that at all."

He was keeping his tone gentle in an effort to calm her. But the fact that what he was really feeling was exasperation only inflamed her agitation.

"Mary had to know," Luke went on. "Especially since I've asked her to come help out in the afternoons. She'll do the cooking and cleaning until you're feeling better."

"I don't want Mary to come." Jenny's eyes grew wider, and wilder. "I don't want any help. I'll be just fine on my own."

"Jenny," he murmured.

"I can do my own cooking," she said, not even hearing him. "I can do my own cleaning. I don't want anyone feeling sorry for me. I'm not helpless. And I won't stand for being treated as if I am."

Through the frenzied haze of her ranting, she was vaguely aware that the Bronco had turned off the main road, that the engine had been switched off. Swiftly, Luke unlatched first his seat belt, and then hers. Then he pulled her against his chest.

She didn't fight him. She couldn't have, even if she'd wanted to. The circle of his arms felt too much like the safe haven she desperately needed to feel grounded and sheltered. Those were the things she'd been missing since she'd awoken in this living nightmare.

"I don't want any help," she said against his chest, but the insistence and creeping hysteria that had been evident in her voice just moments before was all but gone.

"Shhh." He held her tightly. "It's all right. You're okay."

His heart beat against her ear, steady and strong. She inhaled deeply, slowly. He must think she'd gone mad. Crazed out of her head.

"I'm scared." She whispered the explanation, feeling drained and exhausted.

"I know," he told her.

Her body trembled all over, and she sat there for quite a while, pressed against the warm, solid mass of him. Even though it was the middle of summer, a bright and sunny day, she desperately needed the heat that radiated from him. It seeped into her bones, thawing the chill of fear inside her.

He didn't smooth his hands over her face or hair. He

didn't croon soft words. He simply held her, offering her his strength.

She was actually relieved that he remained silent, and finally, she became aware of the chirping of the birds in the trees, the sound of cars passing them every now and then. And when she felt strong enough, and calm enough, she gently pushed herself away from him.

The embarrassment she felt was almost too much to bear as she looked at this stranger who was her husband. But she forced herself not to avert her eyes from his.

"I'm sorry," she murmured.

His dark gaze was so intense it almost felt like a physical touch on her face.

"It's okay."

There was deep emotion in his answer, but Jenny was unable to decipher exactly what he was feeling. He was probably embarrassed for her after that god-awful tantrum she'd just thrown. And she couldn't blame him.

"I have to insist on Mary coming to the house," he told her, quietly, firmly. "I have work to do on the resort. We're cutting trees for four new ski slopes that have to be ready before the first snowfall. Chad and I have to oversee the work crews. I'll be worried if you're alone at the house all day. You understand that, don't you?"

She hated that he was explaining the situation to her as if she were a child. But after the way she'd just acted, how else would she expect him to treat her?

Jenny nodded silently.

"Good." He inhaled, studying her face. "How are you feeling?"

"Better," she assured him. But not quite reassured herself, she repeated, "Better."

He rubbed his fingers over his chin and then rested his

hand on the steering wheel. "You think you feel up to taking another step forward?"

An anxious shiver coursed across her skin. "Another step?"

He shifted in his seat and looked out the windshield. "Yes," he said. "We're home."

She let her gaze follow his, and there at the base of the paved road onto which Luke had turned was a big wooden sign that read Prentice Mountain Ski Resort.

Jenny steeled herself. Gripped the edge of the soft, cushioned seat with the effort of it. She wanted to be strong. Wanted to face all the questions that were waiting for her. Wanted to confront the frightening answers hiding up there on that mountain. But for the life of her, she couldn't help but feel that Luke had just asked her to buckle herself in for another wildly careening rollercoaster ride.

The asphalt road carried them up the mountain for a couple of miles, the densely broad-leafed trees that lined it casting shadows in the late morning sun. Then the woods seemed to fall away and the ski resort stood before her.

She read the signs that directed skiers to the large parking lot to the left, and then Jenny marveled at the huge building sitting a little further up the mountain.

"Does any of this look familiar?"

Luke's soft question drew her gaze. She silently shook her head.

"The original lodge, the portion constructed from rough logs," he said, "was built by my dad and my grandfather. Dad and I added the stone addition about ten years ago."

"Your father and grandfather," she said. "Will I meet them? Are they here?"

"No," he told her. "My grandfather died when I was just a kid. My dad passed on three years ago."

"Oh. I'm sorry." Her attention was drawn to the beautiful lodge. "I'd like to go inside."

But Luke turned onto a small, narrow lane marked Private Drive.

"Let's go to the house first," he said.

She gazed at the resort until it was out of sight, straining her mind for some glimmer of recollection, but failed. Absently, she asked, "So we don't live in the lodge?"

Luke tossed her a smile, and a tiny lightning bolt of thrill shot straight through the anxiety she was feeling over actually facing her homecoming.

"No, we don't," he said. "The business takes a great deal of attention, especially during the height of the ski season. But a person's got to have a place to get away. Even if it is just a quarter mile up the mountain." His smile widened. "Like my dad always said, it's the Prentice way of doing things."

"I see."

"I guess I should warn you," he said. "It's the Prentice *family* home. Chad lives there, too."

She'd be living in a house with both Prentice brothers. She tried to take in the thought without allowing the idea to overwhelm her.

Jenny didn't say a word. She was too afraid to speak. Afraid that if she opened her mouth she might burst into another fit of pure panic.

"It's a big house," he assured her. "You'll have plenty of privacy."

She didn't care if the house was a massive medieval

castle, it still wouldn't be big enough to contain this tangled mess of a situation.

They drove in silence for the few moments it took to reach the house. And Jenny needed every single second to come to terms with the fact that she'd be seeing both of the Prentice men. Every single day.

In the span of what seemed like a short breath or two, the Bronco was parked and Luke was opening the passenger door for her. He clutched her small carryall in one hand and settled the other, in that most familiar manner, on the small of her back.

She hadn't taken three full steps before those dark and sultry swirls began churning deep in her belly. Yet at the same time, the idea of crossing the threshold of this strange house, with all the questions hiding inside, had her heart pounding a furious beat.

She needed to be free of his touch! She needed to find some excuse not to go up those porch steps! Trepidation jumbled her thoughts beyond recognition.

Jenny stopped dead. "I can't," she whispered. "I'm not ready."

Thankfully, Luke's hand swung to his side and she was free. The heated tendrils subsided somewhat, but she still couldn't seem to get her leaden feet to move one inch closer to the front door.

She knew there was pleading in her eyes as she looked up into his face. She wanted him to understand. She wanted him to realize how afraid she was.

"I know this isn't easy for you," he said. "But waiting isn't going to make it any easier."

Jenny blinked. She darted a quick glance at the ground, and then back up to his eyes. He was right. Excuses and postponing weren't going to make her homecoming any easier.

Filling her lungs with a huge, steeling breath, she turned toward the house.

Luke opened the heavy oak door for her and then motioned for her to enter. With her bottom lip tucked firmly between her teeth, she went through the doorway and looked around.

Pennsylvania bluestone covered the floor. Rather than describe the area as a foyer, she would have called it a hallway that ran the length of the front of the house. A gallery, she supposed it was, with tall, narrow windows that let in lots of light. One end of the hall opened onto what looked like a library, a small, cozy room lined with bookshelves. The Queen-Anne-style table and chairs she saw peeking from the room at the opposite end told her that was a formal dining area.

"Well," Luke said, "this is it. Home Sweet Home."

She gazed into the living room in front of her. The lush, dove-gray carpet butting up against the bluestone lent a formal feel that Jenny wasn't sure she liked. She stood there, listening to the quiet.

Luke's hand on her shoulder gave her a start.

"You okay?"

It wasn't until that moment that she noticed she'd been holding her breath, waiting. For what? she wondered.

"Fine," she answered, distracted. The smile she offered him barely curved her lips.

What had she been waiting for? The question continued to niggle.

Had she expected the sight of the house to bring some onrush of memories? An overwhelming flash flood carrying on its swift and turbulent current years and years' worth of mental pictures from the past?

Jenny realized she actually felt disappointed. Again, she

found herself looking all around her, just listening and wondering. Hoping that she would feel some small nuance of familiarity. But she felt no recognition whatsoever. She might as well have been standing in Buckingham Palace, as foreign as this place felt. This house that was supposed to be her home.

"Give it time," Luke said, smoothing his hand over her shoulder and down her arm to her elbow.

He must have read the disappointment on her face. Must have understood her wild, crazy expectation to miraculously regain her memory.

"This might not feel like home to you now," he went on, "but you'll make new memories. You'll have new experiences. Experiences that will turn this house into your home again."

You'll make new memories. *You'll* have new experiences. Jenny studied her husband's face, acutely aware that he hadn't used the word *we*.

He smiled then, and every dark and dire message she imagined he was sending faded into oblivion as the heat of his hand on her elbow seemed to wash across her skin to her forearm, and then her wrist, and then further, until it reached the very tips of her fingers.

This was the first time his body had ever contacted hers, flesh to flesh, skin to skin. Well, the first time in *her* mind, anyway. She'd thought his touch was hot when he'd placed his hand on the small of her back where the fabric of her shirt had been between them, but *this*...

This was fiery. Blistering.

The heat radiating from him became an element with a life of its own, flowing up over her shoulder like some flammable, intoxicating liquid and cascading sensuously down both her back and her chest.

"Do you want me to give you a grand tour?"

Surely he must see, she thought. Surely he must recognize how his touch ignited something in her. Something mysterious. Something frighteningly erotic.

Fearing she was about to burn completely to ashes, or embarrass herself beyond belief, she took a backward step. She moistened her parched lips, her mind whirling as she contemplated a response.

"If you don't mind," she said, surprised by how normal her voice sounded, "I'd like to wander around on my own."

Luke nodded, but his mouth firmed into a straight line. "Whatever you wish." He glanced down at the bag he still carried. "I'll take your things upstairs, and then I'll park the Bronco around back."

His tone wasn't quite clipped, but Jenny could tell her desire to explore the house alone had offended him.

"Well, there she is!"

She looked up and saw her brother-in-law standing by the library door. He'd obviously come from the hallway that led to the back of the house.

Before Jenny could speak, Luke said, "Chad, what are you doing here? You're supposed to be overseeing the work crews up on the mountain."

"Relax," Chad told his brother, tossing out an easy smile. "You're too focused on work. The stress alone is going to give you a heart attack."

"If someone doesn't focus on work, and on getting those trees cleared, the ski runs aren't going to be ready, come winter," Luke shot back.

Irritation emanated from Luke in palpable waves. Jenny watched his jaw tense as he stared at Chad, and she couldn't help but notice how the annoyance he felt turned his features sharp and hawkish.

"They'll be ready," Chad said, seeming not the least

disturbed by Luke's anger. His gaze glittered warmly as he turned it on Jenny. "I just had to be here to welcome you home. How are feeling? You doing okay?"

Jenny was surprised. She'd been dreading seeing Chad again. She'd been confused by the fear she'd felt of him when she'd first awoken in the hospital. But there wasn't a nuance of anxiety in her now. And he seemed so genuinely concerned about her.

"I'm—"

"How do you *think* she's feeling?" Exasperation was clearly evinced by Luke's question. "She's scraped up and bruised. The last thing she needs is to be barraged with a bunch of questions."

Although Chad looked wounded, there was an argument brewing in his brown eyes. "Look, Luke, I only came home to see how she was—"

"But the point is," Luke said, "you weren't supposed to come home at all this afternoon. Someone should be up there minding those men we hired. They're costing us a bundle of money."

"You know they won't take orders from me."

"That's because you don't spend enough time up there—"

"That wouldn't make any difference," Chad said. "They look to you, and you only."

Her gaze bounced back and forth from one man to the other until the bickering made her mind spin.

"It wouldn't be that way if you'd show them—"

"You should have let me go to Olem to pick up Jenny—"

"Please!" She pressed her fingers to her temples.

Silence fell around them like a heavy wool blanket, the sheer weight of it thick and awkward. She hadn't realized how loudly she'd spoken.

A frown planted itself in her brow as she looked, first at Chad, then at Luke. "I'm sorry," she whispered. "I seem to be coming down with a headache. Is there some place I could lie down?"

"Of course."

Both men answered and simultaneously took a step toward her, then froze. The brothers stared, each refusing to back down. Jenny was afraid another shouting match was about to ensue, but then Luke acted. He reached into his pocket and lightly tossed his keys to Chad.

"Please park the Bronco in the garage," he said, his request courteous but edged with steel. "I'll take Jenny upstairs. Then we can go back to work and she can rest. I'll meet you around back at the pickup truck."

She didn't think she could take another round of quarreling, and her expression must have conveyed just that because her brother-in-law's eyes softened.

"You have a good rest," he said. "I'll see you later on at dinner."

Smoothing her hand wearily over her hair, she nodded at him. He left through the front door, and Jenny turned to follow Luke down the hallway to the stairs.

This sudden fatigue sapped her desire to see the house, to explore the rooms for answers to the dozens of questions that had been haunting her for days. All she wanted to do was close her eyes, and escape.

The bedroom was large and had its own sitting area with a plush and inviting couch and matching chair, a small television set, a cherry bookcase and a writing desk. The floor was covered with carpet the color of sea foam, the pale green hue lending a calm feel to the room.

"It's lovely," she said.

Luke set her small bag by the closet door. "No one ever complained about your taste."

"I decorated this room?"

"Uh-huh."

Jenny eased herself down on the very edge of the mattress, smoothing her palm over the pristine white bedspread. She glanced up at Luke and saw that he'd grown utterly still, his eyes riveted to her hand as it slid across the fabric.

The thought hit her like a stone right between the eyes. The bed. She was sitting on the bed they must have shared as husband and wife.

Snatching her hand to her chest, she quickly jumped up. His gaze flew to her face, a mask sliding down over his expression, but not before she glimpsed his pain.

She and Luke had slept together in that bed. Had she taken his brother into this bed, too? The very idea sickened her. Just as, she was sure, it sickened her husband.

"Jenny."

Luke's voice startled her. She looked at him, hugging her arms across her chest. His muscular body was taut and he looked as if he had something on his mind, but couldn't find the words to express himself.

What must he think of her? She was helpless to stop the question from whispering across her thoughts.

"I wish things were different," he said at last. "I'd hoped your homecoming would be..."

He pressed his lips together, letting the rest of the sentence trail off. Reaching up, he raked his fingers through his hair. The breath he expelled was shot through with frustration. "You rest," he told her. "Mary will come later to check on you. I'll see you at dinner."

Then he turned on his heel and left her alone in the peaceful room.

She slipped off her shoes and stretched out on the bed, her chaotic mind a direct contrast to the serene colors and soft fabrics surrounding her. Her greatest wish at this moment was to close her eyes, fly away on the gentle wings of sleep. But her conscious mind had other ideas—ideas it refused to let her ignore.

There were brothers in this house, snipping and snarling like two dogs with one bone. There was a marriage, tattered and torn. And there was a child. Instinctively, Jenny's hand moved to her stomach. A child that two men claimed.

The pivotal point of all these problems was *her*...a woman who had no memory of how any of these situations had come to be. *Lord above, she sent the silent prayer heavenward, how am I ever going to untangle the mess I've made of all these lives?*

Chapter Three

Jenny's eyes fluttered open and a sleepy sigh escaped her lips. The room was illuminated with the soft mauve and gray hues of twilight. She'd slept away the entire afternoon. Her muscles felt languid and heavy, yet her mind was keen, her thinking clear, as if something was about to happen.

Sitting up, she swept back the tangle of hair that had fallen over her face, and before she even had time to draw a deep breath, Luke pushed open the door a crack and peeked in.

His brow creased in an apologetic frown. "I didn't mean to wake you. I only wanted to check—"

"I was already awake," she told him, marveling that she'd awoken with a such a strong feeling of expectation just seconds before Luke had come into the room. Did she have some kind of psychic connection to this man? Some sixth sense that had alerted her to his imminent arrival?

The questions were so silly, they embarrassed her. "I can't believe I slept so long."

There it was again. That devastating smile that sent a jolt of soul-stirring electricity shooting through her. The same smile that softened the harsh planes and hollows of Luke's face, making his handsome countenance even more attractive.

"But you were *supposed* to be resting," he pointed out, his obsidian eyes warm and mellow in the dusky light filtering through the windows.

The concern she read in his gaze made her blood heat. She *wanted* this man. In a purely carnal sense. The thought shocked her. And at the same time the realization made her feel terribly conscious of her disheveled appearance.

"I'm a mess," she murmured, averting her face and combing her fingers through her hair.

"You're beautiful."

The compliment had been whispered so softly, she couldn't even be sure she'd heard him correctly. Jenny lifted her eyes to his and saw a sincerity there that stole her breath away.

She didn't know what to say, how to act, and the silence swelled until it seemed to swirl and pulse with some mysterious energy. Jenny was sure he must hear the thunder of her heart in the utter stillness.

Finally, Luke came further into the room, stopping a few feet from the bed. "How's your headache?"

"Gone," she said, realizing that, for having fallen asleep with such worrisome thoughts, she felt well-rested. "Actually, I'm feeling pretty good."

"I'm glad to hear that."

The silky baritone of his voice sent shivers coursing down her spine. He was close enough to her now that she could smell the warm scent of him, an appealing mixture of woodsy cologne and the clean smell of shower soap. His black hair glistened damp in the fading, rosy glow.

Feeling desperate to break this tense allure threatening to overwhelm her, she reached over and switched on the bedside lamp. But the artificial light did nothing to dissipate the sparks that snapped and crackled in the air.

"Are you hungry?"

How could he ask such a mundane question with all this electricity throbbing in this suddenly-too-small room?

Whether he was conscious of the underlying current or not, his pretense of normal behavior was probably the best way to handle the situation, she decided. She'd simply follow his example.

"I'm starved," she told him, proud of the confident smile she was able to offer him.

Absently, he slid his palm across the front of his shirt. "Mary fried some chicken and made a bowl of potato salad. Oh, and there's baked beans and biscuits, too. And she didn't forget that lemon meringue pie she promised."

She sensed rather than saw his grin as he listed the dinner menu, her gaze glued to his hand where it rested on his broad chest. Even though she knew it was the last thing she should be doing, she couldn't help but imagine how his pectoral muscles might feel under her own fingertips.

Hard and hot, she was sure.

Blinking, she realized that Luke's eyes held an expectant look, as if he'd asked her a question and he was waiting for an answer. Heat suffused her cheeks as she said, "Um, I beg your pardon?"

He chuckled. "I guess the sandman still hasn't let you completely loose."

"I guess." She didn't mind jumping at the excuse he'd

given her for her lack of attention, even though her brain was quick and keen, and had been since the instant she'd opened her eyes.

"I asked if you'd like me to bring you a tray," he repeated. "Or would you rather join us downstairs?"

"I'll come down," she said, sliding to the edge of the mattress. But then she stopped, remembering that Luke had mentioned Mary. "Is she still here? Mary, I mean?"

He shook his dark head. "She had to go fix Bud's dinner." After a moment, he softly added, "Mary was disappointed that she didn't get a chance to talk to you."

Relief flowed through her when she realized she didn't have to deal with yet another new experience. What do you say to people who know more about you than you do yourself?

Evidently, Luke recognized what she was feeling because he said, "It is going to be okay, you know. We're just going to take it one day at a time."

She smiled at him, his use of the plural pronoun making it seem as if she wasn't in this all alone. But she didn't let down her guard completely, remembering how, just a few hours ago, he'd acted irritated, almost standoffish toward her. Luke wasn't going to be an easy man to figure out.

"I don't mean to be timid about meeting Mary. It's just that…" She let the sentence trail, knowing from the look on his face that he understood she wasn't quite ready to take on the whole world.

His black gaze took on a note of warning. "Chad's downstairs. You're all he's talked about today. He wants to see for himself that you're really okay. I hope he won't overwhelm you."

The concern biting into his brow made Jenny feel secure for some reason. After her reaction to Luke and

Chad's bickering this afternoon, she didn't feel that her husband would allow the situation to get out of hand.

Her husband. Thinking of herself as married gave her such an odd sensation. A sensation filled with a multitude of emotions. A sensation she really didn't have time to ponder in depth at the moment.

She hitched up one shoulder a fraction. "I won't lie to you," she said. "I am a little apprehensive."

"There's no reason to be." His smile faded as determination overtook his expression. "You can trust me on that."

This fiercely protective side he was showing made her grow silent, thoughtful. It put her at ease and melted some of the anxiety jittering inside her. She liked the feeling, she decided.

Drawing her spine straight, she didn't smile as she told him, "I do trust you, Luke."

He held her gaze for only a moment, then stuffing his hands into his pockets, he looked away. Was he embarrassed by her admission? she wondered. The thought was heartwarming.

"Let me run a brush through my hair," she told him. "And I'd like to splash my face with a little water. I'll meet you downstairs in a few minutes, okay?"

Luke nodded silently and then left the room.

Padding into the master bathroom, Jenny pulled a clean washcloth from the shelf, moistened it and smoothed it over her face. She scrubbed her teeth and brushed her hair.

Finally, she stared into the mirror at the image that was no more familiar to her now than it had been when she'd regained consciousness four days ago. Jenny Prentice was an unknown entity. As strange to her as Luke and Chad, as Mary and her husband Bud. But in order to get to know the woman staring back at her from the mirror, Jenny knew she needed information. She turned to the door, straightening her shoulders. It was time to come face-to-face with the two men who could give her the facts she desperately needed.

The fried chicken was juicy and tender, and Jenny didn't realize just how hungry she was until she took that first bite.

"This is delicious," she said.

Luke nodded. "Mary's a good cook."

"But so are you, Jenny," Chad told her. "You always loved working in the kitchen."

Jenny tossed her brother-in-law an awkward smile, his compliment making her wonder what kind of meals she used to prepare. Did she favor fancy dishes such as fettuccine Alfredo and seafood paella? Or did she cook simple fare like franks and beans, hamburgers and fries?

"Baking bread was your specialty," Luke said, scooping up a forkful of chilled potato salad.

Chad chuckled. "We always knew when Jenny was upset, didn't we, Luke? She'd be in the kitchen, up to her elbows in flour, bashing the heck out of some bread dough." He grinned at her. "You called it kneading, but Luke and I knew you were imagining one or the other of us under those pummeling fists of yours."

So, Jenny mused, she worked out her aggressions by baking bread. Interesting.

She looked up when Chad chuckled again. "And let me tell you, you baked more bread around here over the past couple of months than you have in—"

One sharp look from Luke, and the rest of Chad's sentence evaporated like water hitting a hot griddle.

"I told you—" Luke leveled a hard look on his brother

"—that we were going to keep the conversation light this evening."

The other man was silent a moment, as though he didn't quite know how to react to Luke's sudden irritation. Then the gaze Chad turned on Jenny lit with rebellion, and a tinge of petulance that reminded her of an overgrown child.

"I didn't mean to stir up trouble," he said to her. Without taking his eyes from his sister-in-law's face, he addressed his brother. "But maybe she *wants* to know what's been going on around—"

"That's enough."

The steely edge to Luke's tone shut Chad up and sent an icy chill coursing across Jenny's skin.

Luke continued to address his brother. "I'd like to remind you that—"

"Big brother Luke has the final say?" Chad interrupted harshly. "That may be true where Prentice Resort is concerned, Luke. But this is a personal matter. One about which I won't be dictated to."

Jenny's nerves began to buzz like dozens of honey bees. Gingerly, she set down her fork. She hadn't expected the evening to take such a bad turn so quickly.

The walls seemed to close in around them. What had Chad meant when he'd said Luke had the final say where Prentice Resort was concerned? She'd assumed the resort was a family-owned-and-operated business. But the thought was a fleeting one at best, the anger building between the brothers overshadowing it completely.

"What I was reminding you of," Luke told Chad, his quiet tone belying the ire simmering just under the surface, "was that Doc Porter told us not to rush things. Jenny needs to rest, to regain her strength."

"What she *needs*," Chad pointed out, "is to discover the truth. The sooner she does, the better for everyone."

Luke wiped his mouth on a linen napkin. "You're bound and determined to fight, aren't you?" Not waiting for a response, he continued. "I won't be bullied into an argument. Not tonight. If you want to hear me yell and curse, I'll be happy to oblige you, little brother. Tomorrow. Up on the mountain where the two of us can be alone. But I won't be putting Jenny through that. Not when everything is so new and strange to her."

The threat of what tomorrow might bring seemed to drain the fight out of Chad, and they ate for several minutes in complete silence.

Jenny felt like a spectator, watching the byplay between Luke and Chad as if they were performing on a movie screen. As though some mysterious writer had concocted the story—*her* story—and she was being kept in suspense over the outcome.

She hated the idea that she was the wedge that was splitting these two brothers apart. She did want to know the truth. She did want to know what had been going on in this house before her accident—no matter how bad that information was bound to make her look. But she certainly didn't want to cause any more arguments between Luke and Chad.

Picking up her glass of iced tea, she took a sip, the dismal thought running through her mind that the fighting was only just beginning. There was no other discernable way around it. Not when she—and her baby—were poised in such a blinded position between these two men.

Luke and Chad tried to make an effort toward civil conversation as they talked of their work up on the mountain. And Jenny tried to pay attention. But the unavoidable thought of her child conjured up questions that simply refused to be ignored.

Had her baby been conceived in the security and warmth of a loving marriage? Or was this child the product of an illicit affair? Clouds of doubt smothered her until her throat seemed to burn with humiliation.

The utter stillness around the table snapped her back to the present. She blinked, looking from Luke to Chad, and then back to Luke. They had obviously noticed that she'd drifted off and gotten lost in her thoughts. There was gentle understanding expressed on her husband's face, but for some reason Chad's open amusement had her feeling like an addle-brained twit.

"Let's have some pie and coffee." Luke smoothed over the awkward moment and rose to begin gathering the dishes.

Jenny made to rise, but Luke patted her forearm.

"Sit still," he told her. "I'll only be a minute."

He left the dining room, his hands filled with a stack of dirty plates and utensils. She was left to stare across the table at her brother-in-law, who made no move to help clean up.

As soon as Luke was out of earshot, Chad leaned toward her and said, "I want you to be wary of anything my brother might tell you about me."

She tilted her head a fraction. "He hasn't said anything at all about you."

"Oh, but he will. I'm sure of it." He lazed against the chair back. "Luke's got some strong opinions where I'm concerned."

His face looked like a wounded puppy's, and Jenny got the distinct impression that he wanted her to feel sorry for him.

"Just keep in mind," he went on, "that anything he says is colored by jealousy."

His blatant implication made her flush deeply.

"Ah, I've embarrassed you."

Jenny's chin tipped up. "I'm afraid, Chad, that the only person who has embarrassed me...is me."

He grinned at that. "You always were one to take full responsibility for your actions." He picked up his glass, but didn't bring it fully to his mouth. "But don't let yourself get too flustered over this...situation. It just might help you to know that Luke's got a few secrets of his own."

She narrowed her gaze at him. "Don't you think it's Luke's place to tell me about any secrets he might have?"

"But will he?"

The question hung in the air as Chad took a drink.

Her husband's face loomed in her mind. He'd seemed so concerned, so sincere, when they had talked up in the bedroom. She'd even gone so far as to tell Luke she trusted him. But now she was discovering he might be keeping things from her.

Luke's got a few secrets of his own. Chad's accusation echoed in her head like the ominous toll of a funereal bell.

"Now, me," Chad said around the small ice cube he rolled in his mouth, "I'll answer any questions you might have with nothing but the honest truth. You can trust me, Jenny."

A chill shot through her like an arctic breeze, freezing her blood. Less than an hour ago, Luke has made an identical claim. Now she was left to wonder if she could trust either one of these men.

"There was a time, not too many days ago—" he hesitated only long enough to give the ice cube in his mouth a sensuous suck "—when you trusted me *implicitly*."

The sexual meaning in his words, in his manner, were unmistakable. Had she really been attracted to Chad? Had they played these sick little flirtatious games right under Luke's nose? The idea that she'd been a party to such behavior turned her stomach. She flinched when he crunched down on the piece of ice.

"All you need to do," he said, his tone silky, "is ask me whatever it is you want to know. I'll tell you the truth. The real truth."

Suddenly she felt all trembly inside, and she identified the fear that was coiling deep in her chest. It wasn't that she was afraid of Chad. No, it was what he might tell her that scared the wits out of her.

She'd thought she was ready. She'd thought she could march down here and face Luke and Chad. Face the facts of the situation. But she'd been wrong. She wasn't ready. She wasn't anywhere near being ready to sort out the fact from the fiction, the lies from the truth. Then there were the secrets to be dealt with.

No, Jenny realized, she simply wasn't ready for this. Icy panic seemed to claw over every inch of her skin. She wanted to escape. She *needed* to escape. To some safe haven. But where?

"Please make my apologies to Luke." Her request came out in a strangled whisper as she shoved back the chair and stood.

Her mind whirled in a frenzy. The utter surprise and distress she saw on Chad's face told her he hadn't realized she'd gone over the edge. Well, she was sorry, but she didn't have it in her to offer him any comfort. All she could think about was getting away. Getting far away.

* * *

Luke carried a tray laden with cups, dessert plates, a carafe of freshly brewed coffee and Mary's lemon pie into the dining room. His whole body tensed when he saw his brother sitting at the table alone.

"Where's Jenny?"

Chad offered his usual innocent smirk. The one that was meant to charm, but did nothing more than irk the hell out of Luke.

"She didn't feel like dessert, I guess," Chad said.

The cups rattled when he set down the tray. "What did you say to her?" He gritted his teeth at the well-practiced expression of guiltlessness on his brother's face.

"I didn't say a thing," Chad said. Then he added, "Nothing that should have upset her, anyway."

"Damn it. I told you not to start in on her. Give the woman a few days to get herself acclimated." Knowing it wasn't in his brother's nature to give anyone anything, he shook his head, murmuring, "Why can't you ever think of anyone besides yourself?"

It was a question Luke often found slipping from his lips. He hated knowing it was his way of refraining from calling Chad a selfish bastard, which was what he *really* wanted to do.

"I only offered to answer any questions she might have," Chad said, his blameless expression turning wounded.

Irritation welled up inside Luke, hot and strong. "Spare me, okay?" He snatched all but one cup and plate from the tray, picked up the knife and sliced a piece of pie. Then he lifted the tray and headed for the door.

"Where're you going?"

Luke's steps halted and he twisted around. "Upstairs."

"But…why?" Chad asked. "She said I was to make her excuses. She doesn't want any pie."

Suppressing his urge to lash out, Luke took a deep breath and counted to three before speaking. "The pie is just an excuse, Chad." He felt ridiculous having to explain the obvious. "I want to check and see that she's okay. I told you she had a bad anxiety attack on the way home this afternoon."

Chad waved his hand in the air. "Oh, it wasn't anything like that. She'll be fine."

"Still," Luke said, "I'm going to see for myself." He made for the door.

"But, wait. What about me?"

Again, Luke paused. "You?" He raised one brow in a mixture of query and impatience.

"You're taking all the coffee." Chad reached for a dessert plate. "How can I enjoy Mary's pie without coffee?"

The roar of frustration pounding in his throat was beaten back with great effort. "There's more coffee in the kitchen," he said, then hastened from the room before he said or did something he'd surely regret.

The anger raging inside him was directed at himself just as much, if not more, than it was at Chad. What kind of man didn't *like* his own brother?

Maneuvering his way up the staircase, Luke pondered his own internal war. Chad was Chad. There was nothing else to say. Luke was stuck. It was all part of the Prentice way, so there wasn't much point wasting time in deliberation.

He shoved the whole concept aside, pausing outside Jenny's bedroom door. His heart twisted painfully in his chest.

It used to be *their* bedroom door. It used to be *their* bedroom. But it had been weeks since they'd shared the master suite. Luke wished like hell he didn't have to admit that to her. He wished like hell he could use Jenny's bout of amnesia to somehow set things straight between the two of them. But he couldn't do that. He'd have to tell her the truth. If he didn't, Chad would make certain she learned of the dismal state their marriage had been in before her accident. It would be best if she heard the bad news from Luke himself.

Apprehension coiled in his gut like a riled cobra as he lifted his hand to rap on the door.

Chapter Four

The room seemed to spin and churn, dip and sway along with the confusion that seemed to be taking her brain on a wild, hair-raising ride.

She had rushed—no, she had *run* to this room, desperately seeking sanctuary. She'd slammed shut the door in some vain attempt to block out everything—the fear, the panic, the doubt, the frustration.

But the things she was trying to escape were inescapable. Because they weren't out there with Luke and Chad. They were in here with her. In her head. In her thoughts.

Jenny sat in the big easy chair, her bare feet tucked up tightly beneath her. One arm was pressed under her breasts, the knuckles of her opposite hand planted firmly against her mouth. Her wide-eyed gaze darted, unseeing, into every corner and cranny in the room. She was caught in the icy clutches of a full-fledged anxiety attack, with no foreseeable way to break its overwhelming grip.

Luke's got a few secrets of his own.

Chad's words kept repeating through her head, like a

mountain echo, bouncing and reverberating until she thought she'd surely lose her mind.

She'd gone down to dinner having come to the relieving conclusion that she could depend upon her husband. She'd decided that her strong physical reaction to him was some internal, intrinsic sign that he was worthy of her trust.

Yes, it had been a shaky trust. Newly born and in need of a great deal of nurturing. But she had grasped it with both hands, nonetheless.

However, that idea was gone now. Dissolved like a piece of loosely woven fabric that had been dipped in strong acid. And she was right straight back to square one, not knowing who to believe or who to rely on.

The knock on the door made her jump, and she barely stifled the groan of apprehension that burned her throat. She didn't want to see anyone. Didn't want to talk to anyone. Why would she, when every word that was said, every phrase she heard was going to have to be weighed for truth and accuracy? She couldn't deal with this. She simply couldn't.

"Jenny, it's Luke."

Her husband's voice came from the other side of the door.

"I want to be alone," she called out, cringing at the high-pitched tone of her voice, which laid bare exactly how panicked she was feeling.

"Please." He paused. "I brought you some coffee. And a piece of Mary's pie."

She didn't respond. She was too busy pressing back the walls of doubt and distress that were closing in on her.

He tried again. "Come on, Jenny. You sound upset. Let me come in. Just for a minute."

He inched open the door enough so that she could see

a wedge of his face. She didn't move a muscle, afraid that if she did, she just might surrender to the impulse to run out into the night.

But where would she go? a tiny voice in her head asked. Supposedly, this was where she belonged.

Evidently, Luke took her silence as permission for him to enter. He approached her, setting down the tray he carried on the table by the chair.

"It isn't good for you to be sitting here in the dark." He snapped on the light to its lowest setting. Then he eased himself down onto the ottoman.

For a long moment, he said nothing. Only looked at her with that dusky, black gaze of his. That gaze that, time and again, churned up sensual feelings in her—feelings she knew she couldn't trust.

Reaching out to her, he took her fingers between his. "You're trembling," he said.

The warmth of his hand was more inviting than a crackling fire on a chilly mountain night. Lord, how she wanted to be held. How she wanted to be rocked, crooned to. But she couldn't allow herself to be taken in by such an invitation, not when her whole world was in such chaos.

Slowly, but firmly, she pulled her hand from his grasp, and for an instant she saw his eyes cloud with hurt. Then he blinked, and the look was gone. She was lucky to have seen the emotion at all. This man seemed to be a master at hiding what he was feeling.

They sat there in the quiet. He, thinking God knew what, she trying hard to contain the anxiety roiling inside her head. She didn't want to show him the weakness she was feeling. Didn't want to put on another "crazy-woman" display as she had this afternoon on the trip home. She could ride out this wave of apprehension. All she needed was a little time. A little space.

Finally, he spoke. "I hate seeing you like this. I hate not being able to help you through this panic that keeps overwhelming you."

Her knee-jerk reaction was to toss him a look of denial. Whether from pride, or the fact that she was trying to hold onto some shred of self-respect, she didn't want him to know she was about to lose control. Again.

Luke shook his head. "Jenny, you can't dispute what you're feeling. Your eyes are wide open and filled with sheer terror. You can't hide it."

He got up from the ottoman, paced several steps away from her, then turned back. "I don't have a clue what Chad said to upset you. I gave him strict orders not to say anything tonight that might distress you." Then he added with a sigh, "But my brother definitely has a mind of his own."

The urge to confront him became more than she could bear.

"He said you had secrets." The words came out whispery and rough, as though her throat were lined with coarse-grade sandpaper.

Luke muttered a curse and his eyes flashed with anger. She knew his fury wasn't directed at her, but that didn't stop her agitation from climbing several rungs on the scale. And this increased state of internal commotion made it easy for the rest of her doubts and fears to slip from her lips.

"He implied that there were things you didn't want me to know. Things you'd be reluctant to tell me. He wasn't specific. There wasn't time for that. But he did state clearly to me that he was the only one I could trust if I wanted to discover the truth. The 'real' truth, as he called it."

She thought it best to leave out Chad's blatant sexual

implication. The tone of his voice alone had been enough to make her overwrought, scrambling for escape. Luke was not the person for her to be using as a sounding board on that subject. That was a problem she'd have to work out on her own.

Silently, she awaited Luke's reaction to her words. Surely he'd lash out against Chad. Surely he'd deny his brother's accusation that he couldn't be trusted. She steeled herself for the onslaught of her husband's anger, waiting for him to attack and condemn and criticize, just as he had been attacked and condemned and criticized.

But the attack never came, and that surprised Jenny more than she was able to admit.

Oh, he was angry to hear that Chad had cast doubt on his character. She could read it in his tense expression, and in every stiff muscle of his hard body. But he continued to study her in silence, until the rigidity seemed to drain from him with a huge, smooth exhalation. The next thing she realized was that a concerned frown had planted itself on his brow.

"I'm not sure there are words to express how sorry I am that you have to go through this," he said. "There's no reason on God's green earth why you should trust my word over Chad's about anything. So I'm not even going to waste my breath trying to talk you into doing it."

Absently, he reached up and combed his fingers through his black hair. "The only solution I can think of is time. Give yourself time, Jenny. Time to heal. Time to…see things clearly."

Now she was frowning. What did he mean? What was he trying to tell her?

"You may feel you can't trust either me or Chad." He shrugged. "Hell, if I were in your position, with strangers all around me, I wouldn't trust a soul." His gaze leveled on her. "But there is one person you can trust. And that's yourself. Trust you own feelings and intuitions. They won't fail you."

"I want to," she whispered. "But sometimes I'm not so sure what I feel *can* be trusted."

Evidently, he knew he didn't need to respond to her statement. Either that, or he didn't know what to say. She couldn't help but wonder if there had ever been a time when she knew this man well enough to know what he was thinking, what he was feeling.

The fact that he seemed to understand her confusion relieved her. Calmed her, actually. But the feeling was short-lived, before a cloud drifted over her thoughts. Could it be that he was focusing attention on her so as not to talk about Chad's accusations? Were the secrets he was allegedly hiding the motivation behind all this concern over who she could and couldn't trust?

Lord, more questions. They were going to be the death of her yet.

The air in the room changed, chilled a degree or two, and Jenny focused her gaze on her husband, saw his body grow taut.

"There's something I need to tell you," he said.

Lifting her chin a fraction, she waited.

He shifted his weight from one foot to the other, averted his eyes and then brought them back to her face. Whatever he was about to say, it certainly was clear to her that he was finding it difficult.

"I'm not sleeping here."

The terse, short sentence had been voiced so quickly, Jenny found herself wanting to ask him to repeat it.

But then he added, "In this room, I mean."

She needed a moment to digest his meaning, and suddenly she found herself blushing. She looked away, murmuring, "I appreciate that. I had worried that you might want to..."

Letting the rest of the sentence die, she pressed her lips together, then found the courage to look him in the eye.

"But under the circumstances, I agree it would be best if you...made other arrangements. Will that be a problem?"

"No, of course not," he told her. "But that's not what I mean. Or rather, you've gotten the wrong impression."

Her embarrassment was totally forgotten now as she looked at him quizzically.

His expression told her he was having a silent struggle with himself. He seemed so averse to explaining himself.

Finally, he spoke. "What I should have said—" he hesitated long enough to draw a breath "—was that I *haven't been* sleeping here. In this room. With you."

Her brows raised of their own accord, her mouth forming a silent O that made her curiosity unmistakable.

Tangling his fingers in the hair at the back of his neck, he grimaced. "I thought you should know."

"Yes," she said, surprised by how unruffled her voice sounded. "That would be a good thing for me to know." Then she asked, "How long had we been having...marital problems?"

His cheeks puffed as he blew out a forceful breath. "Several weeks." His lids lowered in a slow, burdened blink, then he looked at her and clarified, "Actually, it had been nearly five."

Five weeks? She and Luke had slept in separate rooms for five weeks?

"Why?" The tiny question hung in the space between them, then filled the whole room.

She flinched at the disgusted sound that passed his lips. "I wish I knew. I've agonized over how the whole situation came about. I can't explain it to you when I haven't been able to figure it out for myself.''

"But, but,'' she stammered, "what were we fighting about? Surely there were arguments. Angry words. A couple doesn't separate unless there's a problem. What was our problem?''

Luke sighed heavily, shaking his head. "We didn't have that kind of relationship,'' he said. "We didn't fight. We didn't fling mean words at each other.''

After a moment, she softly said, "I don't understand how something like that could happen to two people.''

"Believe me,'' he said, his tone just as confused as hers, "I don't either.'' His nostrils flared as he inhaled. "I hate having to tell you, especially when I'm lacking an explanation. But it was something you needed to know.''

She only nodded.

He approached her. "I certainly don't mean to make this predicament any more complicated than it already is. Hell, that's the last thing I want to do.'' He sat down opposite her on the ottoman. "What I'd like—'' he rested his elbow on his knee ''—is for you to concern yourself with two things, and two things alone.''

Encircling her wrist with gentle fingers, he positioned her hand so it splayed across her own chest, then he eased away from her. She thought it an odd thing for him to do, but she sat motionless.

"First, I want you to worry about you.'' He moistened his bottom lip. "You still have traces of bruising around your eye, and down here on your jaw.''

His fingertips were feather-soft as he brushed them against her face.

"You may not remember it,'' he said, "but you took one hell of a tumble.''

Then he oh-so-gingerly picked up her other hand and placed it against her abdomen.

"And your other concern—" his voice was warm and satiny, like liquid heat flowing through her "—should be the baby."

Luke stood and gazed down at her. "Everything else will fall into place." The barest of smiles played at the corners of his mouth as he added, "Eventually."

He stood looking at her for a long moment, his gaze holding a mixture of sadness and sincerity that struck a chord in Jenny. Then he bid her good-night and left her alone.

She sat for a long time in the big, soft easy chair, one hand pressed against the warmth of her beating heart, the other nestled over her child, thinking about all he'd said. And she finally came to the conclusion that he was right. Her main concerns should be for herself and her baby. Everything else would fall into place. Eventually.

Taking Luke's advice, Jenny spent the next several days indulging herself and her battered body. She slept late every morning, lingered over her morning tea and the newspaper. She found she had a voracious appetite for what was happening out in the world. She supposed this was because she had so little knowledge of her own life, that steeping herself in current events gave her mind something to absorb, something on which to focus.

By noon every day, Jenny was usually showered and dressed and ready to explore. With both Prentice men off working up on the mountain, she had the house and the surrounding resort all to herself. The first couple of days, she stayed close to home, wandering the rooms of the big, rambling house. Yesterday, she'd come across the room

Luke used as his office. And it was here, she was certain, that he was spending his nights.

The daybed in one corner of the spacious office had been neatly made, and she hadn't been able to resist running her hand over the cool, cotton spread. She'd sat in the desk chair, drinking in the scent of him that lingered faintly in the air, remembering the intensity of his obsidian eyes. The same intensity that caused tendrils of desire to curl deep in her belly. The same intensity that made her long to reach out to Luke, to skim her fingertips across his suntanned skin.

She'd pushed those thoughts away, hopped up and gone to check out the view from the office window. The roof of the ski resort had been just visible above the treetops. When she turned back to face the room, she couldn't help but wonder why Luke had been sleeping here for the past five weeks. What had happened between them?

Her husband had claimed there had been no fighting between the two of them. He'd claimed that he couldn't explain their separation.

Was it possible for a married couple to simply drift apart? With no angry words, no quarrels, no discussions regarding the cause? Jenny seriously doubted it.

Was it really that Luke couldn't offer her an explanation? Or that he *wouldn't?*

Finally, the doubts had gotten the best of her and she'd left the office with a firm decision not to return until she felt up to dealing with some answers.

One afternoon, she'd walked to the resort and spent several hours rummaging around the huge log-and-stone structure. The place must be a beehive of activity in the winter months, with skiers coming and going and a huge fire burning in the large, circular hearth. The restaurant kitchen facilities had impressed her, and she'd been surprised to learn from Luke that, during ski season, she was the one who managed the cooking and serving staffs. She'd also found out that she was responsible for creating the work schedules of all the Prentice Mountain Ski Resort employees, and that she signed the weekly paychecks. The thought of herself in such a responsible role was overwhelming, but she realized that she must have been quite proficient at her duties for Luke to have trusted her with so much.

Midway through each afternoon, Jenny found her body and her mind so exhausted that she simply had to lie down for a nap. She had formed the habit of sleeping from four o'clock or so until six, when Luke would wake her for dinner. And it was this habit that had kept her from seeing Mary, the woman who had been cooking all the wonderful meals Jenny had been enjoying.

But after nearly a week of late mornings and afternoon naps, Jenny was feeling more like her old self—

She stopped short, realizing the old adage didn't fit her circumstances at all. She couldn't possibly feel like her old self when she had no idea what her "old self" had felt like. However, indulging herself *had* paid off—her bruises had faded to tinges of yellow around her eye and jaw and the soreness had left her muscles completely.

So today, Jenny was bound and determined to forgo her afternoon nap so she could be awake and alert when Mary arrived. Now that she was feeling physically healthy and strong, she decided she'd like to begin gathering a few pieces of this jigsaw puzzle that was her life. She'd take it slow and easy. She was in no hurry. So that was how Jenny found herself in the sunny kitchen making a pitcher of iced tea as she waited.

Being near Luke aroused such strong and confusing feelings of attraction in her, and talking with Chad only stirred her panic for some reason, so she'd shied away from discussing her past with either of them. However, Mary was supposed to have been her friend, someone who cared about her a great deal. Of course, both Luke and Chad *should* fit in this category, but she had such over-whelming doubt about trusting them. There was one big difference where Mary was concerned. She didn't know about the baby, and that fact meant she was someone who didn't have a motivation to lie. So Jenny decided that spending a little time with the woman would be a great way to start putting together a picture of who Jenny Prentice had been.

Jenny looked up as the elderly woman let herself in the back door. Mary hadn't seen her yet, and Jenny's heart raced.

I don't know this woman, a panicked voice screamed in her head.

"But she knows me," she reminded herself in a whisper.

Jenny forced her feet to stay rooted to the spot, her eyes riveted to the pitcher on the counter. She'd get no-where in her quest to uncover her past if she kept running away from the very people who could help her.

But how should she act? Immediately, she felt awkwardness in every muscle of her body. What should she say?

"A simple hello would be good for starters," she mur-mured.

"A simple hello would be perfect."

Jenny's eyes widened with embarrassment as she swiv-eled her head toward Mary and realized the woman had heard what she'd said.

The smile she managed was shaky, but she offered it nonetheless.

"My land, but it's good to see you up and about."
Mary set a grocery bag on the table and came toward her.

Before Jenny realized it, she was enveloped in a warm
hug that threatened to squeeze the stuffing right out of
her. There was nothing else to do but return the embrace.

The smell of sunshine and flowers wafting around her
lent a secure, homey feeling that Jenny liked. A lot. And
at that very instant, the awkwardness inside her melted
away and she came to the conclusion that Mary was going
to become a precious friend. And if there was something
Jenny needed right now, she knew it was a friend.

Settling her hands on Jenny's shoulders, Mary pulled
back, curiosity lighting her hazel eyes. "Is it really true?"
Mary asked. "Have you really forgotten, er, ah—" she
stumbled over words, looking for one that fit "—everything?"

The only answer Jenny could come up with was a silent
nod. Then she whispered, "I'm sorry."

"Child, you don't have a thing to be apologizing for."
The elderly lady pressed her warm palm against Jenny's
cheek. "It's not your fault. It was that bump on the head
that wiped us all out of your memory." Mary's gaze softened to the point that it grew misty. "Oh, honey," she
cooed, "you must feel so scared and out of place here
now."

This woman understood exactly how she was feeling
and that relieved Jenny enormously. She reached up and
pressed her hand to Mary's.

"I have a feeling," Jenny told her, "that it's going to
get better—no, *easier*—from this moment on."

The two women stood in the sunny kitchen, basking in
the warmth of a budding relationship that for Jenny had
all the promise of a trusting and affectionate bond.

Finally, Mary said, "Enough of this dillydallying.

Those men will be home before too long, and they're going to be hungry.''

She went to the table and began pulling items from the grocery bag. ''I brought the makings for a meat loaf,'' Mary said. Almost to herself, she added proudly, ''Luke just loves my meat loaf.''

''He does?''

''Hmm?'' Mary looked up. Then she smiled. ''Well, he's never complained. And he always takes a second helping.''

Jenny chuckled. ''Sounds like proof to me.'' She moved closer to the table. ''Could I help?''

A hoot of laughter erupted from Mary. ''Are you making fun of me? You know you can cook circles around me. I'm only here because—'' She cut off her sentence as if she'd flipped off a light switch. Then her voice lowered to a solemn tone. ''Oh, child, don't tell me you haven't been working in the kitchen.''

Jenny's averted gaze was enough of an answer.

''You took such delight in cooking and baking,'' Mary said quietly.

She nodded. ''Luke and Chad told me I loved to bake bread.''

''And your bread is so tasty.'' She smacked her lips in a most unladylike fashion. ''Crusty on the outside. Flaky on the inside. Mmm-mmm, good.''

A sad little smile quirked her mouth. ''Mary, I don't remember any of that.''

''Oh, honey,'' Mary said, ''maybe with a little practice, it'll all come back to you.''

Jenny remained silent, refusing to allow herself to hope that such a thing might happen.

With a false buoyancy, Mary blurted, ''Of course you can help me. But don't you go learning any cooking techniques from me." Then she murmured, "Luke will have my head."

Humor dissolved Jenny's sadness and her mouth twitched at the dire tone in Mary's voice.

"I was that good, huh?" she asked.

"Better." Mary waved an onion in the air for emphasis as she continued, "The people around Olem hated to see the restaurant close for the summer. 'Course with all your managerial responsibilities, you didn't do the actual cooking in the resort. You hired two chefs for that. But you *did* create all the recipes on the menu. Original recipes. And you did *that* right here in this kitchen."

Her heart swelled at the respect and pride Mary expressed, but she also felt overwhelmed by how competent the old Jenny had been. Would she ever reach the stage where the people around her would once again admire her achievements? She was too afraid of a negative answer to ponder the question long.

"You're the captain today. What can I do?" she asked, hoping Mary didn't notice her hastiness to change the subject.

"Here," Mary said, plopping the onion into her hand. "Chop this up."

Jenny glanced at the onion and then around the kitchen, a wave of panic coming from nowhere as she realized she hadn't a clue where the cutting board or knives were stored. Mary was quick to come to her rescue.

"I'll get you all set up," she said. She opened one cabinet and pulled out a small, square butcher-block board. Then she tugged open a drawer, extracting a paring knife and vegetable peeler. "Here you are. And you can peel the carrots and the potatoes, too, while I put together the meat loaf."

Jenny settled into the chore of peeling the onion, resting

one hip against the counter. "Mary," she said, keeping her tone as casual as possible, "how close were you and I?"

"Almost like mother and daughter." Mary cracked an egg into the bowl of ground beef.

"Would I have told you if I was having...trouble in my marriage?"

Concern bit into Mary's brow and she rested her hands on the edge of the bowl. "I would hope you would. Why do you ask?"

Jenny hesitated a moment, wondering how much of her situation she should divulge. The idea came to her that she simply *had* to trust someone with her thoughts and feelings.

She moistened her lips, stirring up enough courage to answer Mary's question. "Luke's moved out of our bedroom," she said softly.

The older woman remained silent as she digested this information. Then she said, "I wouldn't call that having trouble in your marriage. Maybe Luke thought that, under the circumstances, you'd be more comfortable with him sleeping in another room."

Jenny could tell by the tone of Mary's voice that the woman was defending Luke's actions.

"I wish it was that simple," she said. "But I found out from Luke that he's been sleeping in his office for weeks."

"Aww, honey, I didn't know. I'm sorry to hear that. Did Luke tell you what happened?"

Jenny shook her head. "He didn't have an explanation."

Then Mary's gaze brightened. "The two of you just had a little spat, is all. I remember when I found Bud's girlie magazines, I was fit to be tied. I was so mad, the poor man didn't even get the luxury of sleeping in his office—he bunked out in the barn!'' Her eyes twinkled. ''He learned real quick to find a better hiding place for his hobby magazines.''

Jenny wanted to laugh at Mary's lighthearted account of her marital problems, but her own troubles were too worrisome. ''Luke said we didn't fight,'' she said. ''He said we never fought.'' She placed the onion on the cutting board and sliced it in half. ''A married couple that never fights,'' she murmured. ''Certainly doesn't sound typical.'' Then she looked over at Mary. ''Does it?''

''Oh, honey, me and Bud fuss at each other like cats and dogs. That's what keeps us young.'' Mary chuckled as she seasoned the meat with salt and pepper. ''But you know, now that I think about it, I never have heard you or Luke say a cross word to each other. You were too busy being happy together. Hand me some of that onion.''

Mary mixed the meat and formed it into a loaf shape.

Picking up a carrot, Jenny ran the vegetable peeler down its length in one long stroke. ''There's something else...'' Her body flushed with the heat of sudden anxiety, and she couldn't bring herself to look up. ''I'm pregnant.''

The silence in the room could have been equated with excruciating pain. Finally, Jenny could stand it no longer and she chanced a quick glance at Mary.

The woman was still, her expression a mixture of bewilderment and concern.

''Jenny, bringing a baby into the world should be a wonderful experience for a woman. But I can tell from your tone that there's something terribly wrong.''

The carrot in Jenny's white-knuckled grip was forgotten as her words turned into a waterfall, roiling and churning one overtop another, as she told Mary all that she knew—how Doc Porter had told her about the pregnancy, how he'd said she'd known about the baby before her accident and how Luke and Chad had both claimed to be the father of her child. When her outburst was over, Jenny was drained and trembling.

Mary looked totally astonished. Her voice was a mere whisper as she commented, "This is just like one of my soap operas." Realizing what she'd said, Mary turned beet red, her eyes widening in horror. "Oh, honey, I'm sorry. I didn't mean—"

"There's no cause for you to apologize for speaking the truth," Jenny told her miserably. Without thought, she went back to the task of peeling vegetables. "What am I supposed to do? Who am I supposed to believe? What's been going on in my marriage? Why has Luke been sleeping in his office? And why would Chad lie about something like this?"

Setting the last of the carrots aside, Jenny began cleaning up the mess she'd made on the counter. "Luke told me not to worry. He told me to focus on getting myself mended and healthy again. Well, I'm all healed. My bruises are nearly gone. So now it's time to look at some of these questions that keep nipping at my mind."

She gathered up all the vegetable peels, dumped them into a plastic bag, secured the top with a knot and set the bag by the back door.

When she returned to the counter, she had every intention of chopping the carrots and potatoes, but the odd look on Mary's face stopped her.

"What is it?" she asked.

Mary pointed at the plastic bag sitting on the floor by the kitchen door. "You remembered."

Glancing at the bag and then back at Mary, Jenny felt her brow crease. "I remembered what? I didn't remember anything."

"Then why did you do that? Why did you put those peelings over by the door?"

Jenny's shoulders lifted in a tiny shrug. "I don't know." Her head tilted to one side as she asked, "Why would I do such a thing? I should have tossed that stuff in the garbage."

Mary's mouth curled into a soft smile. "Whenever I come to visit, you always send me home with all your organic food scraps. For Bud's compost heap."

"I do?" Jenny heard the amazement in her voice.

Nodding, Mary said, "You do."

The questions that plagued her were momentarily disregarded as she pondered her behavior. Bagging up the peels had been an instinctive act. Something she hadn't even been conscious of doing. So it wasn't as though she'd had a recollection. She'd simply performed the task. Like a reflex action. But the fact that she'd fallen into an old behavior pattern had to be a good sign. It had to mean that the old Jenny really was inside her brain somewhere. All she had to do was find her.

A chill raced up her spine. Since this well-practiced habit had revealed itself in so startling a manner, who knew what others might be lurking just beneath the surface? Or when they would appear?

Chapter Five

"What do you think it means?"

Unwittingly, Jenny clamped her bottom lip between her teeth as she waited for Luke to respond. His obsidian eyes were so intense, his expression unreadable, and she laced her fingers together in an effort to quell the overwhelming urge to caress his handsome face.

That very impulse—the one that had her feeling light-headed and giddy whenever she was near him—was going to be her undoing. Each and every moment she was with Luke, she fought the desire to touch him. To stroke his face. To slide her palm over his chest. Rest her cheek on his shoulder.

Blinking several times, she forced herself to focus on the conversation at hand.

Mary had gone home to Bud, and Luke had arrived from his work of clearing trees up on the mountain to say that Chad wouldn't be eating dinner with them. Apparently the younger Prentice brother intended to enjoy an evening on the town, "drinking and carousing" with the work crew, as Luke as referred to it.

"And he wonders why those men refuse to respect his judgment," Luke had muttered. "I just hope I don't get a call from the sheriff."

Jenny had been antsy, barely able to wait to tell Luke about how she'd fallen into the "old habit" of bagging up the veggie peels for Mary; however, Luke's mention of Olem law enforcement had dimmed her excitement.

She'd frowned at Luke. "Does that happen often?" The question had tumbled from her lips before she'd had time to think.

"No," Luke had quickly answered. "I don't want you getting the wrong idea about Chad. It's just that he likes to have a good time. And liquor makes my brother..." He'd searched the ceiling of the kitchen with his gaze in an obvious effort to choose his words carefully. "Aggressive."

Her husband had then asked her about her day, and Jenny had been quick to tell him her news. And now she stood with clasped hands, stifling the curling tendrils of heat that Luke's mere presence induced in her, as she waited for him to tell her what he felt about this subconscious behavior of hers.

"I do remember Doc Porter saying that the human brain is complicated," Luke said.

"It's not like I actually remembered anything," she told him in a rush, "but I *did* something the old Jenny used to do. That's got to mean something." One shoulder lifted a bit as she spoke the last word.

He reached out and enveloped both her hands in his.

Heat. That was all she was conscious of. *His* heat seeping into her skin, radiating across her bare flesh. It felt wonderful. It felt *right*. The excitement already churning deep in her belly spun even faster, metamorphosing into something stronger, something mysterious. She felt as if she was whizzing downhill at breakneck speed, racing toward some secret, hidden goal. Jenny moistened her lips as she waited for, for…something, *anything* to happen.

His gaze didn't waver from her face, but his black eyes did soften. "I don't want you to get your hopes up that this means you're going to regain your memory. Because it may not mean that at all."

She felt her shoulders sag a fraction as disappointment set in.

Was that what she had thought? That because she'd unconsciously performed one, small, formerly habitual act, she'd somehow miraculously regain her memory? Was that what had made her so nervous before Luke arrived? So excited? So anxious to share her news?

Her heart splintered right down the middle as she realized the answer to all those questions was yes. She was amazed that Luke had seen the truth before she had. His understanding of the situation—her thoughts, her rising and anxious hopes—had preceded her own. In fact, she wouldn't have seen it at all, if he hadn't pointed it out to her.

Luke was absolutely right. One tiny subconscious action was not going to open the floodgates of her past.

All at once she realized she was holding her breath. Awaiting what? she silently questioned. She nearly nodded as the answer came to her. The panic. She was breathless as she anticipated being overtaken by panic, the mind-numbing hysteria that never seemed very far away when these small realizations occurred. But the dread didn't descend like a fog as it had so often of late. No, all she felt was a draining disappointment. A bottomless pit of hopelessness that threatened to suck her in.

She leaned into Luke's arms as if it was the most natural thing in the world for her to do. His hands slid across her back, pulling her tighter against him.

"Ah, honey—"

The silky baritone of his voice vibrated against her cheek and she sighed.

"I didn't mean to upset you."

"It's not your fault," she murmured. "You only pointed out the obvious. It's silly of me to think..." She let the rest of her sentence fade into nothing.

He rested his chin against her hair. Standing there pressed against him, Jenny couldn't help but notice how well they fit together. Like a pillow softly cradles a head, her body seemed to conform to his as if they'd held each other a million times in the past. However, to Jenny this was the very first time she and Luke had shared an embrace. A real embrace.

The few moments he'd held her in the Bronco, calming her raging fear, just before they'd driven up the road leading to Prentice Mountain all those days ago, didn't really count in her mind. She'd been too overwhelmed with emotion to remember the incident clearly.

But this? This was warm. And sweet. And secure. Jenny had to wonder how she'd ever imagined that this man couldn't be trusted. In this instant, she'd have trusted him with her every thought, her every fear, her every doubt.

However, she wasn't thinking, or fearing, or doubting at the moment. What she *was* doing was feeling. The heat of his body. The thumping of his heart against his chest. The pulsing of his blood through his veins.

He smelled good, his woodsy cologne filling her nostrils and making her own heart pound a heavy beat. And he felt hard, his firm muscles and broad shoulders clear evidence of his daily physical labor. He was a man any woman would want, any woman would desire. And she was no different from any other woman. She wanted this man. Desired him.

The greedy vines that she'd thought had dried up at the first sign of her disappointment sprouted once again, curling and spiraling inside her like some huge magic beanstalk that offered to take her to some passionate fantasyland.

She'd been aware of her strong physical response to Luke since the very first time he'd touched her in the hospital parking lot. She'd tried hard to put the urges she'd felt for him to the back of her mind. To ignore the hunger that gnawed at the darkest part of her being. But it just seemed that what she was feeling was meant to be. Destiny. Fate.

Ever so slowly, she raised her head from his shoulder, lifted her chin and willed him to look at her. He did, and she knew without a shadow of a doubt that everything she was feeling was clearly reflected in her gaze, plainly written on her face. And the fact that he understood was expressed in his coal-black eyes.

"Heaven help me," he murmured, then he dipped his head, crushing her mouth with his.

His feverish kiss prodded her into motion, and she raised her hands, weaving her fingers into his thick hair, pulling him closer, closer. She was hit by a strange and wondrous wave of unadulterated, sensual emotion. Her blood pulsed through her body like fluid fire, burning, raging, and in an instant, her passion was catapulted to a higher, hotter pitch.

She heard a moan, knew it had come from her own throat, and the sound drove her wild. His kiss was delicious, but suddenly it wasn't enough to appease her deep, aching hunger. She wanted to feel his hands on her bare skin. She needed him to touch her face, caress her shoulders, knead her breasts. It seemed to her that the yearning now threatening to explode inside her had been pent up for years and years, rather than days or weeks. And now that it had found release, her desire couldn't be stopped. Mindlessly, she brought her hands to her collar and feverishly began to unbutton her blouse.

"Wait," he breathed against her mouth, his voice ragged and hoarse.

But rather than heeding his plea, her fingers moved from the facings of her blouse to his shirtfront. With quick, fervent motions, she unfastened one button after another.

"Stop, Jenny. Please." He encircled her wrists with his hands and held her tight. Then he paused long enough to tip back his head, close his eyes and inhale a deep breath.

She felt him shaking with the effort he was putting into dousing the flame burning inside him, and suddenly she felt terribly ashamed.

What was she thinking? Had she actually been about to undress herself? If he hadn't stopped her, she'd have stripped herself *and* him right here in the middle of the kitchen.

The realization dissolved the desire that had fogged her brain. Her cheeks and neck burned with humiliation. How could she have lost control to that extent?

"I'm sorry," she whispered huskily, and then she bit down on her still-moist bottom lip, intent that the tears of humiliation burning her eyelids would not fall.

He expelled a sigh. "Don't," he told her, his tone almost rough. He gently cleared his throat then ran his tongue over his lips. "Don't apologize. I've been wanting to do that for what feels like...ages."

She blinked once. "You have?"

The small laugh that erupted from deep in his chest was tinged with chagrin. "You haven't noticed?"

His question made her smile. "No," she said, dipping her head shyly, "I've been too busy fighting my own battles with that huge monster named—" Her face flamed with renewed heat but she refused to let embarrassment keep her from finishing her sentence. Looking him directly in the eyes, she boldly finished, "Desire."

He let his hands slide up along her forearms until he cupped her elbows. The pads of his fingers skimmed back and forth on the sensitive skin of her inner arms, and Jenny felt her heart trip against her ribs. It would be so easy to lose herself once again in the passionate frenzy that lurked just beneath the surface of her barely contained emotions.

Although it was evident that he tried to control his tone, his voice was still quite raw as he said, "You can't know how good it is for me to hear you say that."

The moment seemed charged, heavy with electricity that sparked and flashed in the air around them.

"I've tried to control my body's response to you," she told him. Then she gave a quick, ironic exhalation. "Maybe what I'm feeling for you is just another instinctive habit." Her lashes fluttered down as she asked, "Tell me…were we compatible in the bedroom?"

She'd expected him to laugh at her teasing query. She'd certainly meant to make him smile. To somehow lessen the tense current that made the atmosphere in the kitchen feel like a swollen, overblown balloon.

The hurt she saw in his eyes when she finally looked at him surprised her.

"What?" she asked softly. "What did I say?"

He shook his head. "Nothing."

But his expression of displeasure belied his answer. He stepped away from her, obviously trying hard to don an emotionless mask. However, he wasn't succeeding.

She felt chilled now that they were no longer in contact. Crossing her arms over her body, she slowly rubbed her hands up and down them. She couldn't allow him to hide his feelings from her. Not after the kiss they had shared. She had a chance to get closer to Luke. Not taking advantage of the moment would be a sin.

"Please, Luke," she said. "I want to know."

He'd averted his gaze, remaining stubbornly silent, when it dawned on her what the problem was.

"Ah—" she nodded "—I see. You don't like the idea that what I'm feeling for you is *physical*. You want my response to you to be more…meaningful."

Bingo. She'd hit the bull's-eye. She read it in his gaze, in the sudden awkward stance of his body.

Still, he didn't respond, only studied her with those deep, powerful eyes that made her feel censured, made her want to give him excuses.

"What do you want from me?" she asked. The question held no accusation. In fact, her tone was gentle as dandelion fluff. "What are you hoping for?" she went on. "Do you want me to say that I love you? I don't know you, Luke. You're a stranger to me."

His jaw tensed and he looked away. "I know that."

He rubbed the first two fingers of his right hand over his mouth, obviously contemplating what to say; however, Jenny couldn't help but wonder if the memory of their kiss was forcing its way into his thoughts. It certainly was burned into hers.

You'll make new memories. The promise he'd made to her the day she'd returned to Prentice Mountain echoed through her mind. Luke had been right. She *was* making new memories. And the memory of the kiss she'd just shared with him was one she never wanted to forget.

"It's just that—"

The sound of his voice snapped her back to the present.

"—it's been so hard," he said, "knowing what we had together. And seeing all that disappear. As if it never happened."

There was pain etched in the planes and angles of his handsome face, and Jenny wanted to reach out to him. But she didn't, because just as the idea of comforting him formed in her mind, she was struck with guilt that seemed to come out of nowhere.

"I'm sorry," she breathed. "I've been so focused on myself this past week. I've been thinking of nothing but my own wounds. The ones on the outside—" reaching up, she touched the side of her eye that had been swollen and bruised "—and the ones on the inside. My fears and doubts about…everything…"

"Jenny."

He tried to stop her with an upraised hand, but she wouldn't be stopped.

"I should have realized that I wasn't the only one who was suffering." Her guilt suddenly seemed to weigh a ton. "I should have seen that I wasn't the only one who was dealing with a new situation."

"But that's exactly what I wanted you to do," he told her. "I told you to concentrate on getting yourself healed. You needed to focus on yourself." Then he softly added, "And the baby."

It was all she could do not to give in to her mothering instinct and place a protective hand over the child nestled inside her. However, she resisted the urge because of Luke. She clearly saw that he was suffering with the weight of the doubts he carried about the baby. Yes, he'd claimed to be the father, but she saw the shadows of skepticism in his gaze. He fought it, but the question showed. And it pained him. Because she was unable to assuage his doubts, she decided to let the subject rest. Shining light on the questions of her fidelity and the baby's paternity would only build up the very wall she was trying to tear down between herself and her husband.

"Well, we're okay," she said, wanting to assure him where she could. "The baby and I are in fine shape."

"You're sure?"

She shrugged. "I'm sure about myself. I feel great. And I've had no sign that the baby isn't okay. I have an appointment to see Doc Porter next week."

Luke bobbed his head slowly up and down, and the tension around his eyes and mouth seemed to dissolve as though her assurance was finally relieving him of worry he'd held onto for some time.

The atmosphere between them began to ease and Jenny found it less difficult to pull air into her lungs. She enjoyed a moment of relaxed silence.

Finally, she said, "Luke, don't you think it's about time we talked?"

"We talk," he said.

But the fact that his gaze was fixed on a spot just over her shoulder was quite telling to her.

"We talk every evening at dinner."

A laugh escaped her. "You call that talk? I'm so afraid that you and Chad will discuss the past that I do my best to hide behind all those current events I keep spouting off about." Again she chuckled. "I've apprised both of you of every church social and bake sale in the county. And I forced you to listen while I prattled on about the latest

scandal in our nation's capital, and about the serial bank
robber in Philadelphia.''

''And it's been very interesting, too.'' Luke kept a
straight face for all of three seconds. Finally he gave in
to the smile he was holding back. ''I guess you can tell
that I was *allowing* you to hide yourself in all that news.''
His chuckle subsided as he admitted, ''I guess in a sense,
I've been hiding, too.'' His chest expanded as he gave a
surrendering sigh. ''You're right. It's time we talked.''

They sat facing each other across the dinner table,
Mary's meat loaf steaming on a platter between them.
Jenny served them both a helping of creamy mashed potatoes and sweet carrot coins. Hot biscuits slathered with
butter rounded off the meal to perfection.

''Tell me about us. How did we meet?'' Jenny forked
a carrot, slipped it into her mouth and slowly chewed. She
barely tasted the tender vegetable, so anxious was she to
hear what Luke was about to say.

His hesitance in answering her caused her brow to wrin-
kle, but she waited patiently. Recounting their past was
going to be a monumental task for him, she was sure. She
needed to take it slow and easy, giving him all the time
he needed.

Finally, he said, ''We met through Chad.''

Her brows rose almost of their own accord. The fact
that his brother had brought them together bothered him.
She could tell from the look on his face.

''You went to college with him,'' Luke went on. ''Villanova University.''

So, she was an educated woman. Questions swam in
her mind—what was her major…had she enjoyed attend-
ing school…had she earned a degree? But she firmly set
her mind on sticking to one topic at a time, and the current

subject was one of utmost importance: her and Luke's relationship.

"I would guess I came here with Chad to ski." Her conjecture was spoken as a statement, but she did wait for him to confirm or refute it.

He nodded. "For four winters running. There were about eight or ten people in Chad's group of friends. The whole rowdy bunch of you came as often as your class schedules would allow."

The corners of Jenny's mouth pulled back in a grin. "Sounds as though you didn't like us being here. Noisy group of college kids. Where we a royal pain in your backside?"

"No," he said. "It wasn't that."

But she was very aware that he didn't say what it *was* that had him feeling so tense about how they first met. And he was tense. She saw it in the rigid set of his shoulders. The tautness of his jaw. Another clue was that he hadn't yet taken a single bite of his dinner.

Jenny thought it best to veer away from this part of their history. She could always come back to it later.

"How long have we been married?"

A smile crept across his lips. "We'll celebrate our fifth anniversary in a few months."

"Five years together," she murmured. "Were we happy?"

"Very." He picked up his fork, cut a square of meat loaf and ate it.

Jenny thought it utterly amazing how the shift in the direction of the conversation transformed his demeanor. One minute he seemed to strain and deliberate over his words, the next he was quite relaxed. She hadn't a clue why that would be. Maybe they'd had a rocky courtship. Then again, maybe he'd swept her off her feet in a whirlwind romance and he found telling her about it a little embarrassing.

"So how are we together?" she asked, smearing a pat of butter on a biscuit half. "What kind of things do we like to do together?"

"Well," he began, "during winter we work. Hard. From the time the sun comes up 'til it disappears we're both over at the resort working our tails off. It's an honest living, though. Satisfying." He grinned. "And we make enough money in four months—five if the weather holds—to last us all year."

"We only work five months out of twelve?"

He laughed. "We only work *hard* for five months. With a resort the size of ours, there's plenty of upkeep all year round," he said. "And this off-season we've dedicated to putting in the new ski runs. But usually we can be a little lazy in the summer."

His gaze took on a suggestive gleam that nearly caused her to blush.

"We take lots of long walks." His voice dropped. "Just the two of us. Up there. On the mountain."

The hungry expression on his handsome face led her to imagine all sorts of erotic preoccupations they might have found when they were all alone and hidden by the trees, brambles and bushes on Prentice Mountain. The idea of making love with Luke out in the wide-open spaces of nature made her heart thud against her ribs.

She set down her fork and gazed up at him through half-closed lids. "So we take lots of walks, do we?"

He studied her with his sexy eyes. "*Lots* of walks. It's our favorite pastime."

Now her cheeks did flame with color because it was so very obvious that their most preferred diversion had nothing whatsoever to do with strolling in the woods. Finally, she tossed him a seductive grin. "I sure am glad to know we get plenty of...exercise."

His head lifted as he laughed. Then he reached across the table, covering her hand with his. "We were very happy together."

"So what went wrong?" The question tumbled from her lips so quickly it startled her.

His sigh was huge and seemed to be tinged with a mixture of regret and sadness. He didn't release his hold on her hand; if anything, his grasp tightened as he asked, "Can we put off discussing that?" Before she could answer, he continued, "I know our separation needs to be talked out. You need to know everything that happened. But I feel like we're just getting started here, and I'd like to spend some time on the good things we had together."

He did have a point, she realized, and she was in no hurry here.

"Okay," she agreed softly. "How about if you tell me about your dad? You told me he died three years ago, which means he was living when you and I were married. Did he like me? Did we get along?"

"Dad loved you," he said. "Just like you were his own daughter." Then he chuckled. "Of course, you did everything right."

"What do you mean?"

"You loved the outdoors," he began the list. "You loved to ski. You told him Prentice Mountain was your favorite place in the whole, wide world. And you worked your fanny off to make his resort a success." He let go of her hand and laced his fingers behind his head. "Oh, and you could cook. In Dad's book, you were A-okay."

She smiled, pleased to know that she'd gotten along with her father-in-law.

"Did I ever meet your mother?" she asked.

Luke shook his head. "She died, oh, let's see…it's been fourteen years now. She was out with my dad on a snowmobile. They ran off the trail. Dad blamed himself. And I don't think he ever forgave himself, either." His gaze glazed over as he became caught up in the memories. "I was twenty. Chad was only eleven. It was a good thing Chad was still young enough to need some raising. I know he was what pulled Dad through that awful time."

"It had to have been an awful time for all of you," she said. Then realizing the age gap between the brothers, Jenny did the mental calculation. "There's nine years between you and Chad?"

Luke snapped out of his sad reverie with a single blink. She'd struck a nerve.

"Uh-huh." His chin lifted a fraction. "There's nine years between you and me, too."

She sensed a hint of challenge in his tone, as if he expected her to be shocked, or at least upset by the notion. Jenny supposed this subject had been a sore spot between them before they married. She also wondered which of them had thought their age difference mattered. Had she been the vain type of woman who would have been bothered by such a trivial thing? Suddenly, she was sorry she'd even brought it up.

"So your father had a rough time of it when your mom died?" she asked, hoping to soothe the feathers she'd so obviously ruffled.

He was silent a moment. Then he nodded. "I am glad that Dad could focus his attention on Chad." The chuckle he expelled didn't hold an ounce of humor. "He might have given Chad too much attention, but…"

His thought faded, and Jenny couldn't help but think the asides he continued to utter were revealing something of importance.

"You said that we met through Chad." Absently, she toyed with her napkin. "How did he feel about you marrying one of his *rowdy* friends?" She grinned when she used Luke's description of Chad's group of college pals.

He straightened in the chair, his hands coming down to his sides. "He didn't know."

Her brow tensed with bewilderment. "How can that be?"

There it was again, she noticed. That awkwardness. That hesitation.

"He wasn't here," he said after a pause. "The day after graduation, Chad hit the road. He left. To see the world."

Resentment coated his tone like thick paint.

"But didn't you..." She stopped, then corrected herself. "Didn't *we* contact him about the wedding?"

"We didn't know where he was. He was traveling around." Luke lifted one shoulder. "Like I said. He was seeing the world."

She shook her head, her laughter clear evidence that this simply didn't make sense to her. "He didn't call? Or write?"

"No."

"But why?" She sat back.

Another shrug. "That was the way he wanted it, I guess."

"I don't understand. Did he have an argument with your dad or something? With you? What happened?"

"I'll tell you what happened, he—"

He hacked off his own sentence with the force of a machete blow. Bitterness oozed from him like blood from a wound, and Jenny was taken aback to the point that she didn't know what to say to him.

His nostrils flared slightly as he inhaled deeply and then

exhaled through his taut lips. The action seemed to drain at least part of the volatile emotion from him.

Finally, he said, "Chad didn't know about our marriage until about five months ago, when he returned home from his travels in Europe. He didn't seem to mind that you married me. But then again, maybe he did. I really don't care one way or the other. But if you're curious about why he left the mountain, or why he stayed away so long, or why he didn't contact us, I think it would be best if you ask Chad those questions."

His face was void of emotion, his small oration measured and tightly controlled.

Planting her elbow on the table, Jenny rested her chin in her palm, wanting to seem relaxed in the sudden stiffness that had sprung up. "I hope you don't mind this observation, but…you don't seem to like your brother very much."

He got up and gathered his plate, his utensils and his glass. "As a matter of fact, I do mind."

Over at the sink, he rinsed the dishes and then loaded them into the dishwasher. The silence was awkward and she didn't like it at all.

"I'm sorry," she said, following his lead and clearing up her dinner dishes. "I didn't mean to offend you."

"You didn't offend me," he said. He turned off the spigot. "It's just that…" He paused, busying himself with tucking his fork and knife in the dishwasher's utensil rack. "Look," he said when he straightened, "Chad is Chad. He is who he is. That can't be changed. You'll understand that more once you've spent some time with him." Then he softly murmured, "Or maybe you won't understand."

Another one of those asides, she noticed. She was quickly learning about her husband's style of communication.

He went back to the table and picked up the meat platter. "The fact is, Chad is family. I don't think it matters much if I like him."

"Of course it matters," she told him. "A person may not have a say in which family they're born into, but you certainly should have a choice regarding who you spend your time with. Or who you spend your life working with. Or who you live with." She took the damp dishcloth, swiped it once across the table and then stopped to look at him.

"I don't understand why," she continued, "two men who obviously don't get along would choose to coop themselves up in the same house." She bent to finish wiping the tabletop. "I sit here with you two at dinner every night. I see the way you barely speak to each other. Barely look at each other." She shook out the cloth over the garbage can and then placed it neatly by the sink. "I mean, I can see there would be difficulty about working together, seeing as how the two of you are joint owners of the resort, but—"

"I own the ski resort."

His voice was loud enough to make her jump, and she was astounded by the annoyance expressed in his sharp, narrowed gaze.

Then she remembered the sarcastic comment Chad had made about Luke being the final decision-maker at the resort. She hadn't commented then, and certainly didn't feel it prudent to do so now, but it was evident that ownership of the resort was a sore spot between the brothers.

"But as long as Chad wants to work here, I'll make sure there's a job for him. Like I said, he's family. And we take care of our own. It's the Prentice way."

He set down the bowl of the vegetables with such force that some of the buttery juice of the carrots sloshed over the edge. "And did you ever stop to think that my brother and I experience a little awkwardness at the dinner table because *you* are sitting there between us? *You*, the woman who is carrying a baby that one of us has fathered?"

He stalked out of the kitchen muttering something about paperwork that needed doing, and Jenny was left standing there feeling chagrined, and very much put in her place.

Chapter Six

Standing in the inky shadows, he watched her sleep. Her hair glowed golden in the moonlight slashing across the pillow. If he got closer, he'd smell the heady aroma that he knew was Jenny's alone. He wanted desperately to stroke her alabaster skin, kiss her full, sensuous lips.

She belonged to him.

She slept on her back, one arm splayed above her head, the other tucked beneath the peach-colored blanket. Her chest rose and fell with each gentle breath. Sweat broke out across his brow and prickled his upper lip as he fought the urge to approach the bed.

One of her satin-covered breasts was exposed by the coverlet, her tawny nipple a faint shadow against the thin material of her nightgown. The sight of it, the thought of it caused him to grow hot and rock-hard in his pants.

She belonged to him.

His gaze darted to the window as the night breeze ruffled the curtain. But in an instant, his unblinking eyes once again latched onto her supine form.

What he wanted to do, what he *should* do, was fling the blanket aside, trap her body beneath his, tug the thin straps of her nightgown over those milky shoulders, kiss every inch of her naked flesh, make her call out the name of the man she loved, the man she wanted. His name. He could force her to confess she wanted him. He'd done it before, he could do it again.

She stirred, sighing softly. The sound made his palms grow damp. His mouth watered profusely as he imagined all the pleasure he would take in her. Because he would have her. In the end, she would be his.

She belonged to *him*, damn it! And he would have her. If he had to lie, cheat or steal. He would have her.

And all that came with her.

Jenny dressed quickly the next morning, tugging a royal blue tank top over her head and slipping her legs into a pair of white denim shorts.

She felt a little tired, having had a terrible time falling asleep last night. She'd tossed and turned as Luke's harsh words had echoed in her mind over and over again.

How could she have forgotten that *she* was the cause of the rift between the brothers? She, a woman pregnant with the child of one or the other of the men, was the reason there was resentment and hard feelings between Luke and Chad. The reality of it had eaten at her until she'd eventually dropped off to sleep.

She rubbed a washcloth over her face, brushed her teeth, ran a comb through her hair, all too conscious of the guilt weighing heavy in her stomach. Remorse creased the tiny patch of skin between her eyebrows as she applied a touch of mascara to her lashes.

Maybe she should leave Prentice Mountain. She picked

up a small tube of colorless lip gloss. Maybe both Prentice men would be better off without her.

But where would she go? she wondered.

As she smoothed her pinky finger across her lips, Jenny's mind was invaded by thoughts of Luke and the kiss they'd shared. She surrendered to the aggressive invasion, happy to yield to the memories of his hot, moist mouth on hers. She trembled as she remembered the feel of his thick, silky hair between her fingers.

Yes, he'd tasted wonderful, felt amazing, but it had been the molten desire that had radiated off him—desire he felt for *her*—that had affected her most. There had been no doubt as to just how much he'd wanted her. He'd quaked with the effort of reining in those feelings. The idea that her husband was drawn to her thrilled her. She couldn't lie to herself about that.

However, she was disturbed by the deep-seated fury that simmered just below the surface in Luke. She'd seen him nearly explode in the hospital emergency room when Chad had claimed to be her baby's father. And she'd seen his anger appear again last night before he'd stomped off to his office.

She understood his rage, his humiliation, his frustration, understood what he felt toward her might be justified. But what she couldn't figure out was why a man, who felt so many complicated and angry emotions toward a woman, could also feel desire for that same woman—desire that burned as hot as a roaring inferno.

The face that stared back at her in the mirror was not one that would stop traffic on Main Street in Olem. The features weren't uncomely, but neither were they stunningly beautiful. Her looks were not the kind that would send a man over the edge with passion. Her eyes were a plain brown, although the tawny brows that framed them were nicely shaped. Her nose was straight. Her mouth, with its full bottom lip, did look quite pleasing tinted with this sheerest of glossy color.

Her hair was her best feature, she judged, narrowing her eyes at the mirror, as she combed the soft tresses curling at her shoulders and the wispy strands bordering her face. Its upkeep took little-to-no effort on her part, just a quick shampoo and blow-dry, and fate had blessed her with an awfully nice color, a golden hue bringing to mind sunny days, or dandelions, or the soft, fluffy down of baby chicks.

Jenny chuckled and put down the comb. Yes, she had nice hair, but she couldn't imagine Luke losing control of himself over a simple thatch of curls.

Depends on where those curls are located.

The erotic thought shocked her, but not enough to keep a delighted laugh from bubbling to the surface. What was it about her husband that always caused her mind to turn to sensual—or were they *sexual*—thoughts?

Luke had never answered the question she'd posed to him about the state of their sex life. No, the conversation had veered in another direction before he'd had the chance to respond. But if the kiss they had shared last evening had been any indication, Jenny knew the answer to her query.

She left her bedroom, trying to push the cheek-warming memories aside by focusing her thoughts on the kitchen and the coffeepot. But questions regarding Luke and their relationship continued to seep into her brain like water leaking through the space at the bottom of a closed door.

Since she was no dazzling beauty, what was it about her that Luke found so attractive? She mentally shrugged. Everyone knew that love was blind. She'd read Shakespeare's *A Midsummer Night's Dream*. The looking glass of love painted a distorted image for anyone who gazed through it. Lovers rarely, if ever, saw the truth when they looked at each other. The passionate perception was so much more pleasing, even if it was less revealing.

She wondered what Luke saw when he looked at her. And further, which of Luke's faults and imperfections didn't she see, didn't she perceive, because of the strong attraction she felt for him?

When the stunning realization hit her like a swiftly swung baseball bat to the kneecap, she stopped on the stairs, blinking several times.

She remembered reading Shakespeare's play. During a high-school literature class, she'd given an oral report on the romantic farce.

For the pure joy of it…simply because she *could,* she stood on the steps, her heart racing with excitement, and relished the memory of Helena, who was in love with Demetrius, who was the suitor of Hermia, who was in love with Lysander. The story was a romping merry-go-round of misplaced passion as she remembered it. Her favorite character of the tale had been Titania, Queen of the Fairies, who loved all things beautiful but ended up suffering a bewitching affection for the donkey-headed Bottom. It had been this ridiculous, potion-induced devotion of the Queen's that had convinced Jenny all those years ago that love truly was blind.

She remembered! Standing in front of the class. Nerves dancing in her stomach like a dozen twirling ballerinas. Shaky hands as she held her note cards. Her silent prayers that she'd pronounce the characters' names correctly.

A memory. A real, solid memory from her past.

This was no obscure, subliminal action. This was no vague habit that had been performed subconsciously.

The picture in her head was genuine. In her mind's eye,

she could see her index cards, the blackboard, the huge windows, the desks, the students. Even though it was only a tiny flash, an instant from her youth, she remembered it.

Her legs felt suddenly weak, as if they wouldn't hold her. If one memory was tucked away in her brain, others must be there also.

Of course, she couldn't name the state or city, the school or teacher, but she did recall *something,* and that was all that mattered at the moment. It was enough to give her hope. Real hope. Not the false sense of expectation that had been provided by the incident with Mary in the kitchen, but an honest-to-goodness feeling that, just maybe, her memory *would* return to her.

She had to tell Luke about this. She had to find him and tell him about this recollection.

Then she remembered his angry words as he'd left her alone in the kitchen last night. He didn't want to have anything to do with her. Not while their lives—*all* of their lives, hers, his and Chad's—remained twisted in the tangled triangle of suspected secrecy, lies, distrust and deceit.

Her heart fell. She had no one to share her excitement with. No one to talk to about her recovered flash of a memory.

Mary! Jenny's spirit's soared. She'd tell Mary all about her experience this afternoon.

Feeling once again lighthearted, Jenny almost skipped down the remaining steps, her thoughts again on a steamy cup of coffee.

The sight of Luke leaning against the counter, sipping from a mug, made her stop short in the kitchen doorway.

"How come you're still here? Shouldn't you have left for work already?" She heard her accusatory tone of voice, although she hadn't meant to sound that way at all. His presence had simply taken her off guard.

"Good morning to you, too," he said smoothly.

Looking down at her bare toes, she murmured, "I'm sorry. It's just that I've gotten kind of used to having the house to myself at this time of the morning."

She lifted her chin. He studied her so intently with his dark-as-night eyes that she had to force herself not to look away.

A now familiar heat began to build inside her. Darn it! Why couldn't she control her libido when she was in this man's presence? Her attraction to him seemed to have a life, a mind, of its very own.

Finally, he said, "I've been working seven days a week for the last two months. I decided to take the day off. Besides, it's Sunday. Even God got to rest on Sunday."

She listened for his sarcasm, looked for his anger, but all she heard was a touch of humor in his voice, all she saw was a teasing glint in his gaze. He had obviously lost all the anger he was feeling toward her when they parted last night. Jenny shook her head, feeling that she'd never figure this man out.

Luke took another swallow of coffee. "And the way those men partied last night in Olem," he said, "not one of them, including Chad, is going to be worth a tinker's damn today."

She nodded. "I hadn't even realized it was the weekend." She felt sheepish as she made the admission. "The days tend to run together when you're on your own."

His gaze wandered to her lips and stayed there a few seconds longer than it should have, and the heat inside her intensified a few degrees.

"We'll have to do something about that, won't we?"

His voice was so very like a physical caress that, for

an instant, Jenny could almost have believed he'd actually reached out and touched her.

The air grew stifling and taut, and she had to make a conscious effort to drag it into her lungs. She felt overtaken by a sudden nervous energy, a heightened sense of awareness.

Desperate to ease the tensions she'd created between them last night, she blurted, "I'm sorry for what I said about you and Chad. I was way out of line and..." Seeing him shake his head, she let the rest of her thought drift away, unspoken.

"It's okay," he assured her. "I was wrong to have reacted the way I did last night. I want you to be able to say whatever's on your mind."

After a moment, she responded, "Well, what's on my mind now is your day off. I'm glad you're taking it. You deserve it. You work too hard."

They gazed at each other in the silence that settled upon them, the atmosphere becoming tighter and tighter by the moment. Jenny felt as if they were attached together by an invisible, overstretched band that pulled them, tugged them inexorably together. However, she hadn't moved a fraction of an inch and was forced to wonder if this strong pull was the result of her overactive imagination, or if he felt it, too.

Every muscle in her body seemed to bunch and tense with the need to move, and finally, when she could stand it no longer, she went toward him. At the last moment though, she lost her nerve and veered to the left where the coffeepot sat waiting on the counter.

"Let me just grab a cup of coffee," she said in a rush, "and I'll go back upstairs, out of your way."

What she'd planned to do once she'd reached him, she hadn't a clue. All she did know was that she'd lost her nerve to perform it, and she couldn't stand there in that smothering room another second.

"Wait."

His fingers encircled her forearm, as hot as an antique iron that had just been removed from the fire. She looked at his hand, sure her skin would be scorched to the bone when he released her.

Standing motionless, her coffee cup poised in the air, Jenny waited with her heart thumping a hard, steady rhythm. Her expression was expectant, yet she felt almost frightened of what might happen next.

Did he have to touch her? The feel of his skin on hers was like dry kindling being added to the glowing embers of a fire.

"I have an apology to make, myself," he told her.

"An apology?" There was surprise in her raspy whisper. She couldn't begin to imagine what he might have to be sorry about.

Slowly, he nodded his dark head twice. "I blamed you last night for the ill feelings between myself and Chad. Well, the reality of it is, the situation we find ourselves in is only partly responsible for the rift in the relationship I have with my brother."

His jaw tensed, and although the heady desire Jenny was feeling was shorting out the circuits in her brain, she could tell that this subject was difficult for Luke to discuss.

She forced back the urge to cup her palm against his cheek, feeling that action would be highly inappropriate at the moment. When it was clear to her that he didn't intend to elaborate any further, she couldn't help but ask, "Would you tell me about it?"

He deliberated, his eyes revealing a clear reluctance. After heaving a sigh, he said, "Okay. I'll tell you all about it." He paused the briefest second before adding, "If you'll spend the day with me." One corner of his mouth tipped up in a most charming smile. "Let's pack some sandwiches. Take a walk. Nobody ever said you couldn't have a picnic in the morning, did they?"

The most carnal part of her mind focused on one word alone. *Walk.* Luke had told her last night that taking walks used to be their favorite pastime, and both of them had known he wasn't speaking of walking at all...what he'd been speaking of was making love. Could it be possible that he was asking—

"No, no," he hurried to assure her.

Luke evidently read the look on her face, a mixture of emotions, pervaded by sudden uncertainty, but also including an expectancy that was laced with undeniable hunger.

His black eyes became clouded and unreadable. "Unless, of course..."

She began to stammer and blather like an idiot chicken squawking uncontrollably when a fox was discovered in the coop.

His eyes twinkled with merriment and he quieted her by placing his index finger against her lips. "I'm joking." He chuckled. "When I asked you to go for a walk with me, I meant a *walk.*" He laughed again. "Just a walk."

Having misinterpreted his invitation—even for a moment—left her more than a little embarrassed. Her sheepish grin was slow in coming and was a ridiculous attempt to lessen her discomfort. But what she really wished she could do was diminish the disappointment she felt at hearing that a walk and a picnic breakfast was really all Luke was looking for.

"All right," she said softly. "I'll make some sandwiches. Peanut butter and jelly okay with you?"

"That sounds fine," he told her, "but I'll make the sandwiches. You need to go get yourself ready."

Bewilderment creased her brow. "But I am ready. I'm all dressed and ready to go."

His grin broadened and he let his gaze fall pointedly to her feet. She looked down, and then she wiggled her bare toes self-consciously.

"Oh," she said. "I guess I do need to go put on some shoes first."

She hurried off, his soft laughter causing tiny, heated sparks to explode deep inside her.

The western hemlocks shot skyward, thick enough in some places along the trail to block out the sun. Spruce trees added a startling dash of blue-gray to the lush greenery of the maples, beeches and dogwoods. The mountain laurels and wild azalea bushes, long past their spring flowering stage, added their own distinct shades of green to the forest.

Jenny heard a rustling in the underbrush, but didn't turn her head quickly enough to get a glimpse of what animal was scurrying to escape her and Luke's presence. The sound had been reminiscent of a small creature, though, a chipmunk, maybe, or a squirrel or rabbit.

The air was clear and clean and fresh, and she inhaled deeply as she hiked with Luke up the mountain trail. Yes, her thigh muscles screamed, but it felt so good to be out and moving. Really moving her body. Before today, her exercise had consisted of exploring the resort buildings. This excursion had her blood pumping, her skin tingling. Of course, these bodily responses had absolutely nothing to do with the man at her side. The silent sarcasm made her suppress a grin.

"You okay?" Luke asked.

"Uh-huh."

"You sure?" He slowed his long-legged gait and shifted the small wicker basket he carried to his other hand.

"Yep." She hoped the smile on her lips would reassure him further. When the concern on his brow didn't lessen, she said, "Would you stop worrying about me? I'm fine."

His pace slacked even more and he observed, "Your breathing is heavy."

Her smile metamorphosed into something akin to a spontaneous, wicked grin. "Sometimes it's good to breathe heavy."

Flirt! Flirt! her brain silently teased her, and she was surprised that it hadn't sounded like the admonishment she knew she needed but almost an egging-on. Tantalizing encouragement.

Luke's gaze grew dusky with understanding. Grinning, he held out his hand to her. She slipped her fingers into his palm, and they continued up the mountain.

Before long, he said, "This looks like a good spot, don't you think?"

"But we haven't gone all that far," she said. "Don't stop on my account."

He chuckled. "What are you trying to do, walk me ragged? It's my day off, remember."

"Well, if you're going to be such a Weak Willie about it," she said, holding back a laugh, "I guess this spot will have to do."

"Weak Willie?" He set the basket on the grass. "Where'd you come up with that?"

Jenny shrugged. Then her gaze narrowed on him. "Why? Did I use it before my accident? Have I called you that before?"

Luke shook his head. "Never heard you use the term before today. I just wondered…"

The rest of his thought died away when he noticed the look on her face, registered the obviously frantic tone of her voice.

"You've started remembering things."

There was no way she could have misconstrued his statement as a question, so she gave a slow, confirming nod.

"What?" he asked her. "What have you remembered? Your accident? Do you know why you went to Simon's Point when you knew it was dangerous?"

At any other time, she'd have taken great interest in the questions he was bombarding her with. In fact, his inquiry would have caused her brain to churn, so intent had she been lately on putting the pieces of her past together. But she was so eager to share her recollection with him that she rushed full-steam ahead without actually hearing what he'd said.

Her quick recounting of her Shakespearean memory almost had her bouncing up onto her toes with excitement.

Finally, she said, "I know it's not much. A small memory. But it's *something*. And it was so clear. I could recall all the characters' names and standing in front of the class to give my oral report. Don't you think this is a good sign?"

He shook his head up and down. "I'm sure it is. It has to be, doesn't it? Should you call Doc?"

"Oh, I don't think it's that important," she told him. "I'll tell him when I go into Olem next week." Once her frenetic thoughts calmed, she took a moment to ponder. "What did you say before?" she finally asked. "Something about my accident?" Her head tilted as she added, "What's Simon's Point? Or rather, *where* is it?"

"Come," he said, reaching his hand out to her. "Sit down with me and I'll tell you."

He led her to a log that had fallen ages ago, the bark long since worn away, its dark surface providing a smooth, perfect seat for them.

Once the two of them were settled, side by side, Luke said, "Simon's Point is on the west face of Prentice Mountain. When Chad first arrived home and it looked like he was here to stay, you and I talked about building a house. A home just for the two of us. You suggested Simon's Point. We looked into it and found that the Point was too full of shale to make it safe to build there. There was even a little blasting done to see how deeply the stone went. Shale is crumbly, sort of like pea stone. The blasting only made the Point more dangerous."

His jaw muscles tensed. "Chad and I found you, unconscious, at the bottom of the Point." He rubbed agitated fingers across the back of his neck. "I actually laughed at Chad when he suggested we look for you there. 'She'd never go to the Point,' I told him. But we'd looked everywhere for you. And you'd been missing for hours. I finally allowed myself to listen to my brother, and we drove to Simon's Point." He shook his head, his voice softening. "The rest is history. I'll be forever grateful to Chad. He should get all the credit for us finding you. If I'd had my way, you'd probably have—" A disgusted hiss passed his lips. "I don't even want to think about it. But it's time this was admitted. Out in the open, so you can hear."

Sliding his fingers under her chin, he tipped up her face and forced her to look into his eyes. "My stubbornness, my jealousy, my anger...my weaknesses nearly cost you your life, Jenny."

She reached up and enveloped his hand in both of hers.

"You're being too hard on yourself. You said you didn't believe I'd go to Simon's Point. You said I knew it was dangerous."

He pulled his hand free, refusing to be consoled. "It wasn't just that that kept me away from the Point. I didn't want to go because…"

The deep, steeling breath he took told Jenny just how reluctant he was to go on. Then a determined resolve lit his ebony eyes.

"Because," he continued, "Chad was the one who suggested we search there. If anyone else had made the suggestion, I probably would have gone in a flash."

Guilt weighed heavy in Luke's tone—guilt that had Jenny feeling ultracurious about the meaning behind what he was telling her. She simply waited for him to elaborate, knowing he had every intention of doing so.

His exhalation was filled with regret. "Just looking at my brother makes me angry." His voice was a mere whisper as he said the final word, as if feeling the emotion somehow made him less human. "I've never allowed myself to admit this to anyone. Not even you, my wife, the person I'm closest to. But the truth is—" his gaze clouded with immense pain "—I've been jealous of Chad for so long."

Her eyes rounded with alarm as she took his statement to heart. "Then I *did* do something to make you jeal—"

He lowered his eyelids, cutting off her words with a weary shake of his head. "This started way before you came into the picture. Years ago, actually. When I was just a kid. And Chad was just a baby." He smoothed his palms up and down his jean-clad thighs. "You see, mom suffered several miscarriages before she became pregnant with my brother."

His eyes took on a far away look, telling her he was lost somewhere in the past.

"My parents gave him so much attention when he finally arrived. Before Chad was born, I used to get the attention. I played Little League in the spring, peewee football in the fall. But suddenly there was a baby in the house, and he seemed to be the excuse my parents used for everything. We couldn't go see the Fourth-of-July fireworks display in Olem because the show started too late for the baby. We couldn't watch the Firemen's Parade because it was too windy for the baby." He blinked slowly. "I was miserable after my brother was born."

She ached to reach out and touch him, but she didn't. "A little jealousy between siblings is natural. Especially since you'd had your parents to yourself for so long before Chad was born."

"But I was his big brother," he said, disgust aimed at himself evident in his tone, in his hardened gaze. "I had no business feeling anything but love for him. He was nine years younger than I. I was old enough to know better." Then he murmured, "I *am* old enough to know better, yet I can't help feeling what I feel."

"Luke, it sounds to me that what you felt..." She paused, and then corrected herself, "what you *continue to feel* toward Chad, wasn't and isn't all your fault. Your parents seemed to have forgotten that they had an older son."

But he didn't even hear her, so locked up was he in the prison of his guilt.

When Luke's mother died, Jenny surmised, the situation must have only worsened for him. She guessed that was what he'd meant when he'd said his father had given Chad too much attention after his mom had passed away.

As if reading her thoughts, Luke said, "After Mom

died, Chad became my dad's whole world. When Chad went off to college, Dad was so proud. But when he left Prentice Mountain to travel around Europe, Dad was devastated. I tried to console him, tell him that Chad would be back, that we'd all work the resort together just like he dreamed we would. But he was never the same. Then he died.''

Looking at her handsome husband, the sun glinting off hair so black it radiated blue, Jenny couldn't help but feel that something was missing. That Luke was leaving out some part of the story.

From everything she'd learned, Luke was a levelheaded man. Filled with simmering anger at times, yes, but he simply didn't seem the type to harbor resentment against someone who didn't deserve it. And from what he'd said, he honestly felt that Chad didn't deserve the bad feelings Luke had for him. So what was missing? she wondered. Why was Luke blaming his brother for the treatment he'd received as a child when he should be blaming his parents? These were questions she simply didn't have answers to.

I tried to console him, Luke's words whispered through her mind, *tell him that Chad would be back, that we'd all work the resort together just like he dreamed we would.*

Ah! Jenny almost nodded at this revelation. One thing was very clear now. Luke was trying to make a dream come true. The only problem was, it wasn't his dream he was striving for, it was his father's dream.

The more she found out about her life, her husband, this family, the more complicated the puzzle seemed to become.

Chapter Seven

After making what he'd obviously felt was a huge admission, Luke had grown quiet. Jenny knew he was like a long-distance runner who had finally crossed the finish line and, drained and weary, was in dire need of rest. She'd been happy to respect his silence.

The sun's rays filtered sporadically though the thick, leafy canopy overhead. Birds chirped high in the tree branches, and Jenny came to the slow, languorous, almost lazy, conclusion that there was nothing more relaxing than nature. The heat of the sun on her skin, the heady aroma of pine wafting in the light breeze, the high-pitched scolding of the goldfinch. She sighed contentedly, enjoying the mountain morning.

She'd eased herself onto the grass, using the log as a backrest, and Luke wasn't long in joining her. Yes, she'd been intent on the trees and sky, the small scavengers searching the underbrush, but she was also acutely aware of her husband at her side. The solid mass of him just a fraction of an inch away.

Before long, the natural world surrounding her seemed to recede into the distance as she became more and more focused on Luke. Jenny knew it was crazy, but the heat radiating off his body seemed warmer than the summer sun. Reclining her head to one side just a tad closer to him, she sat utterly still and smiled when she heard the sound of his rhythmic breathing.

Those oh-so-familiar tendrils of heated desire swirled in an unhurried, arousing dance, dipping and swaying deep inside her. She'd grown to love this feeling. The warm and delicious wanting that pulsed in her blood, twirled in her stomach.

Sure that he'd drifted off into a light doze, she cast him a sidelong glance and was startled to see his eyes wide open, staring straight at her face.

Heat suffused her cheeks and she tossed him a quick smile before looking away. Just how long had he been studying her? The question unnerved her, sending her thoughts into sudden disarray.

"Would you like something to eat?" she asked, her eyes searching out the basket that sat on the grass just out of arm's reach. A bubbling titter erupted seemingly out of nowhere, and Jenny was terribly embarrassed to admit to herself that it had come from her throat. Thinking to camouflage her discomfort, she blurted, "There's nothing like a peanut-butter-and-jelly sandwich to take you right back to your childhood."

She sensed him stiffen, and realizing the words that had just tumbled from her lips, she turned horrified eyes on him.

"I'm so sorry," she murmured. "After what you told me, revisiting your youth is the last thing you want to do."

For the sole purpose of having something to do, she

leaned forward, meaning to pull the small picnic basket to her.

He stopped her by placing his hand on her shoulder.

His fingers spread over the cotton fabric of her tank top, but the palm of his hand came into direct contact with her skin. Flesh to flesh. Her blood throbbed thickly through her veins and she was sure her brain wasn't getting the oxygen it needed to create clear, concise thoughts.

"Relax," he told her, gently guiding her back into a reclining position against the smooth log.

But it wasn't until he took his hand off her that she realized she really wasn't going to faint. It was only his nearness, his touch, that had her feeling light-headed and dizzy. For days and days, she'd been aware of his effect on her, but her body's reaction to him was, at this moment, stronger than ever before.

Focus on something else, *anything else,* her mind directed. Concentrate on the wind blowing in the treetops. Forcing her eyes shut, she realized that, at the moment, there was no wind. The birds, then. Listen to the birds. Latching onto one particular sound, she chanted to herself. What kind of bird made such a shrill, busy call? What kind of bird made such a shrill—

"A bobolink."

Her lids whipped open, and she turned to stare at him. Had she really asked the mantralike question aloud?

She nibbled her bottom lip for the span of several heartbeats. Then she said, "You must think I'm an idiot."

His gaze roved slowly over her face. "I think you're beautiful."

The resonance of his voice was like black silk, deep and whisper-soft, the caressing sound of it setting the nerve endings all across her skin aflame. The tempo of her heartbeat accelerated until the pounding on her ribs grew almost unbearable. Breathing became difficult, and she found herself deliberately drawing air in through her mouth and forcing it slowly out her nose. The last thing she wanted to do was lose control.

"Listen," he told her, tilting his head a fraction toward the birdcall. "That's a meadowlark."

She paused and looked upward. "It sounds so—" she searched for an appropriate word "—melodic. Beautiful."

She actually started when he slid the backs of his fingers up along her jaw. But when he lightly traced the outside curve of her ear, she smiled, relaxing against, and relishing, his touch.

"Not nearly as beautiful as you," he said.

He withdrew his fingers and she felt bereft with regret and longing.

"I get near you," his said, his tone a rusty whisper, "and all I want to do is touch you."

Leveling her gaze to his, she saw in his eyes a silent question, a pleading for permission. The flames of desire inside her leaped, licked, burned her with a wanton need to feel his hands, his mouth, on her.

She gave him the barest of nods and he reached out, grasping her shoulders. His biceps bunched and she marveled at the ease with which he lifted her. It was as if she weighed no more than a sparrow as he pulled her onto his lap. She tumbled against his chest, steadying herself by splaying her hands on his shirtfront. His heartbeat pounded steady and strong against her palm, its rhythm blending with the vibration of hers.

His jaw was smooth as he rubbed it across her cheek, his hands sliding along her back, tugging her into an even closer embrace.

"Just let me hold you a minute."

His voice grated against her ear, rough as grit, yet saturated with a craving that refused to be denied.

Nestling her face between his collar and the curve of his neck, she pressed her nose, her lips against his heated skin. He smelled like the woods surrounding them, warm, earthy, alive. She parted her lips, slid the tip of her tongue across his flesh and tasted the slight tang of salt.

He groaned, turning his head to kiss her bare shoulder. Then he pulled her away from him, slowly, slowly, sliding his hands up her arms, over her shoulders, her neck, cupping his palms on either side of her face. His dark and probing gaze darted from her mouth to her nose, her hair, her forehead, finally coming to rest on her eyes.

She felt as though she were teetering on the edge of a most passionate precipice, yet rather than being afraid of the lofty altitude, she felt exhilarated, excited. She *wanted* to let go, she *wanted* to fall right into the sensuous depths of his arms, of his black-as-midnight gaze.

Her breathing came in fits and gasps, her chest rising and falling with her ever-building hunger. Gathering his shirtfront in her fists, Jenny decided she could wait for his kiss no longer. She leaned toward him, intending to press her mouth to his. However, with one quick and gentle twisting motion, Luke pressed her down into the soft grass and hovered over her as she lay on her back.

The gasp that caught in her throat expressed both her surprise and her disappointment. She needed to feel his lips on hers. She needed to taste him. Now.

"Kiss me," she whispered, not the least embarrassed by the desperation she heard in her own voice.

"Not yet." His fingertips traced her cheekbone. "Waiting will make it better." He loosened her hold on his shirt, lifting her hands up over her head, resting them on the grass.

Jenny tried to relax, even though she wanted nothing more than to tug him to her frantically, to kiss him, to touch him.

The pads of his fingers ran lightly, languidly over the inside of her upper arm, the contact with this supersensitive skin producing an excruciating pleasure that radiated throughout her entire body. She closed her eyes, relishing the shivers that coursed across her flesh. This simply had to be the most wonderful torture imaginable.

His hand slid lower, lower until his thumb grazed the underside of her breast. Immediately, her nipples budded into tiny stones, straining against her bra and the thin blue cotton of her tank top. She heard his breathing grow ragged, but she didn't raise her eyelids. This sightless state, being unable to anticipate his next move, yet knowing he was watching her body's every reaction, heightened her desire to an unbearable level. If he didn't kiss her soon, she would surely shrivel with this need and die.

Sliding his palm over her breast, he gently kneaded, once, twice. His face was close to hers, his sweet breath caressing her cheek. She fought to keep silent, resisted the urge to beg for his kiss. She also battled to keep her eyelids closed. She wanted desperately to see the fire she knew must be in his eyes, but this blinded, passionate encounter was terribly erotic.

His lips grazed her jaw. She nearly cried out, turning her mouth in that direction, lifting up, reaching for him, but he was too quick for her.

In her dark world, her skin was hyperalert to any sensation, so that when he kissed her neck, concentric shivers coursed across every inch of her flesh. His mouth was warm, his tongue moist. His kisses blazed a fiery path down onto her chest where the scooped neck of her top exposed plenty of her for him to savor. And savor, he did.

Finally, when she could no longer stand the urgency thrashing, hot and heavy, in the deepest depths of her being, she opened her eyes wide. Raising her arms, she laced her fingers behind his head and guided his mouth to hers.

Luke started to whisper her name but was only able to speak the first syllable before their lips clashed in a fervid explosion that rocked Jenny to the very center of her soul. The moments that followed were a blur of pure carnal pleasure. They feasted on each other, both doing their best to satiate their own gut-burning hunger. There simply was no other way to describe it.

Before Jenny was aware of it, Luke's shirt was completely unbuttoned, and she ran her fingertips over the broad expanse of his chest. Her own top was bunched up, her lacy bra unfastened, her breasts exposed to his ravenous gaze, his luscious, supping mouth.

His hand slid silkily down her abdomen, skimming beneath the waistband of her denim shorts, the very tips of his fingers tracing a delicate line along the elastic of her underwear. She moaned, urging him on. He unbuttoned and then unzipped, laying open the facings of her shorts. Then his hand hovered a scant inch above her body as he paused to gaze at the creamy lace of her panties. There wasn't much visible, only a small, V-shaped slice, but his voracious gaze lingered on the scrap of fabric, causing the most feminine part of Jenny to grow moist with aching need.

Without conscious thought, she curled her hips, the slow, lustful thrust bringing her body once more into contact with his fingers. His eyes widened, and he sucked in a gulping breath. He looked up at her face. The passion exposed there was bold, raw.

His head blocked out the sun as he bent to kiss her on

the mouth. The tiny circles his fingers drew around her navel were made with the lightest touch, and Jenny's abdominal muscles tightened.

Slipping her palm overtop his, she guided him down, down, down, the excruciating slowness only intensifying the moment. Their eyes were riveted to the sensual journey their hands were making. He was so close, Jenny saw, her heart racing with anticipation. So close to possessing that most feminine part of her.

Luke stiffened for only a fraction of a second. The fiery trail of their hands ceased as she sought his gaze. Bewildered by the apology she saw there, she frowned. He blinked once, looked back down where her hand rested on his, but Jenny could tell that something had severed the thin, intense thread that had so completely connected them, nearly making them one, for the past few moments.

"What is it?" she asked. "What's wrong?"

"Nothing."

But the small utterance grated against his throat as though it actually caused him physical pain. The sensual haze fogging her brain quickly evaporated when she realized he was avoiding looking her in the face.

"Luke?" She lifted her hand an inch or so from his, aware of the summer air filling the space between their flesh.

Still he did not meet her gaze.

"It's nothing," he insisted, making an obvious effort to recreate the heated mood that had wrapped them like a thick cloak by taking her hand in his, lifting her fingers to his mouth and softly kissing her knuckles. But his momentary hesitation still lingered, lurking like a dense thundercloud on the horizon.

The fact that he didn't retrace the white-hot trail their hands had made down her belly wasn't lost on her. The last spot he'd touched before freezing had been her lower abdomen. His doubt about the baby was what had made him pause. That was clear to her.

"This isn't going to work." She tugged her hand from his and struggled to sit up.

"Wait, Jenny." He leaned over her, the sheer bulk of him keeping her from rising more than an inch or two. "I want this to work. We can make it work."

The awkwardness that came over her was huge, disturbing, and she didn't like the feeling of being trapped under him when these tumultuous emotions were threatening to drown her. Shoving at his shoulder, she pushed him far enough away that she could scramble to her knees.

"Can't you see that's impossible?" she cried, straightening her clothing as best as she could.

Why did these stupid, annoying tears have to well up now? she wondered, dashing a particularly fat one away with a quick swipe of the back of her hand.

"We can't make *anything* work," she went on shakily. "Not when the paternity of this baby is in question."

"It's not in question," he stated, his black eyes glinting with a stubborn gleam.

For a moment, the chirping of the birds filled in the tense silence between them.

"I see the doubt in your eyes," she told him quietly. "I see it in your face. You can't even touch me, for heaven's sake, the doubt is eating at you so. You can't hide what you're feeling." She studied him for a moment. "You might want to lie to yourself, but you can't lie to me. I can read you like a book."

"You always could," he murmured before glancing away.

He looked so defeated that it tore at Jenny's heart. She reached out and touched his forearm with her fingertips.

"Luke," she said when his gaze was once again on her face, "I can't deny that we have something between us. Something wonderful. Something that's begging to be explored. Something that promises beauty. Joy. Ecstasy." Her imagination silently implored her to elaborate further, but she refused to dwell on a blissful sexual future with her husband, not when that future depended so heavily on discovering the past.

"But don't you see that we can't allow ourselves to be swallowed up by what we're feeling?" she asked. "Not when there's someone else who needs to be considered."

An angry shadow crossed his face. "Chad." He nearly spit out his brother's name.

She slowly shook her head. "I was thinking of the baby. Don't you want to be able to hold this child and say for certain whether you're a father or an uncle?"

His expression cleared and she got the impression he was trying to tell her he didn't care one way or the other, but she was very aware that he remained silent.

Her spine straightened and she narrowed her eyes. "It matters to me." She stood up and snatched up the small basket. "It matters to me *a lot.*"

Luke caught up with her, gently taking the basket from her. Then he took her hand in his as they walked along.

"It'll all work out," he promised.

However, the uncertainty lacing his declaration weighed heavy in every step of her journey home.

The sun was high in the sky when the house finally came into view. The temperature had climbed steadily, and combined with the physical exertion of the walk, Jenny found herself feeling sticky, uncomfortable, exhausted. All she wanted to do was have a cool shower and lie down in her quiet room for a while.

They couldn't have been fifty feet from the house when Luke stopped and turned to face her.

"I have something I need to say," he told her.

She suppressed a weary sigh, feeling too tired, emotionally and physically, to rehash this colossal, seemingly unsolvable, dilemma they found themselves ensnared in.

His voice grew quiet as he continued, "We've grown closer, you and I. And in trying to sort things out, we've discovered that we have something." His smile bordered on a grimace. "Granted, it's almost purely physical. But it's something. And through this attraction we feel, maybe we can grow closer still."

He bent over, planting a soft and sensuous kiss on her cheek. Then he whispered, "I'm going to hold tight to that."

Her heart fluttered.

Both of them turned when Chad called out from the front porch. Luke's grasp on her hand tightened and Jenny wondered if she had imagined the possessive gesture, because her husband's voice was amiable as he greeted his brother.

"You've had a few phone calls," Chad told Luke when they got closer. "Messages are on your desk."

"Thanks," Luke said. Turning to Jenny, he said, "I'll see you later, okay?"

She nodded, suddenly invaded with dread at the prospect of being alone with her brother-in-law.

The front door hadn't even swung completely shut behind Luke when Chad's gaze sharpened with open accusation.

"What was that all about?" he asked. And before she could answer, he threw out, "Where have you two been?"

She didn't stifle the sigh that had built up deep in her

lungs. "Chad, I'm hot. And I'm thirsty. And I don't feel like fighting."

Brushing past him, she went up the steps and into the house.

"What was he doing kissing you?" he asked, following close on her heels.

Jenny couldn't deny the awkwardness that crept over her like the long, slow squeak of a rusty door hinge. She tried to consider Chad's side of the issue.

She understood him being upset at seeing Luke holding her hand, kissing her cheek. But she refused to deny what she felt for her husband. She wouldn't flaunt the sexual attraction she and Luke felt for each other. Doing so would only hurt Chad, and that wasn't her intention. But neither would she twist the truth. The sooner Chad knew how things stood, the better for him, Jenny decided.

"He's my husband, Chad," she said, going straight to the back of the house, to the kitchen. "Husbands kiss their wives."

He reached out, grasped her shoulder and spun her around roughly. "Luke shouldn't be kissing you."

The edge in his voice sent a small jab of fear slicing through her. "It was nothing," she said, hating herself for lying when she'd just promised herself she wouldn't.

"Nothing?" He looked pointedly at the basket that Luke had obviously left on the counter on his way through the house to his office. "You took food on your little morning excursion. The two of you had a happy little picnic."

"Stop it, Chad." She shrugged his hand from her shoulder, trying to calm the apprehension that was climbing her spine one vertebra at a time. "If it will make you feel any better, we didn't eat a bite. Have a sandwich, if you like."

Rather than calming the man, her remark only seemed to agitate him more. "If you didn't eat," he said, "what *did* you spend your time doing?"

Filthy innuendo dripped from his sarcastic question. Understanding his anger was one thing, being the brunt of his foul accusations was quite another.

"I don't owe you any explanations."

She turned to the cabinet and pulled down a glass.

"You owe me plenty."

"Oh?" She whirled on him.

His eyes were hard slivers of bronze, his full bottom lip tight and cruel. He shook his head. "Bouncing from one brother to the other like some whore."

The anger and annoyance left her as if someone had pulled the plug on a giant drain. Left behind were the very dregs of some horrible emotion, a mind-numbing sludge of sensation that shocked the words right off her tongue.

Was he right? The silent question taunted her as she stood there, motionless, the glass still in her hand. How close to correct was Chad's assessment of her character? Was this the awful truth that Luke had put off discussing with her? Was she the kind of woman who could hop from one man's bed to another's without a thought for hurt feelings or painful consequences? The questions sickened her.

She blinked, focused on her brother-in-law's face, saw his eyes grow wide with apology.

"I'm sorry, Jenny." He took the glass from her hand, led her to the kitchen chair and guided her into it. Then he crouched by her side. "I should never have said that. It was pure frustration talking. You've got to believe me. I would never hurt you. Never."

Her mouth was so dry, her thoughts so scattered. She couldn't seem to gather her wits about her.

"It's just that you made a commitment to me," Chad said. "Just a few days before your accident. I haven't said anything because Luke told me to give you time to heal. Give you space to deal with your amnesia. And now I find out that he's trying to move in on you. He's trying to win your affections when he told me to back off. He's manipulating us."

"No," she whispered feebly. "It isn't like that at all. What Luke and I have feels too…natural…."

"Look, Jenny," he said, cutting her off, taking her fingers in his desperate grasp. "You have to give me a chance. I have to let you know that you have your back to the rainbow. What you're facing is the storm. Yes, it may be intriguing—beautiful, even—but it's full of dangerous lightning, frightening thunder." He squeezed her fingers, his brown eyes pleading with her. "You have to turn around, Jenny. You have to get a glimpse of the gorgeous colors you and I had together before you choose to live the rest of your life in the rainstorm you and Luke had together."

She remained silent, not knowing what to say.

"You and I made a baby, Jenny. A *baby*."

Chad pressed his free hand to her belly, his intimate touch making her so uncomfortable she had to force herself not to squirm under his palm.

"We made a baby together," he repeated. "And you need to think about our child before you go making decisions that are going to affect all our lives. We're a family, now. A family of three. You need to think about that. Remember it." He stared at her for a long moment. "You had feelings for me, Jenny. You did. And that alone should make you see, make you *agree,* that I deserve a chance to tell my side of the story. *Our* story."

Jenny felt shaky, faint. The man kneeling by the chair had caused her nothing but awkwardness, discomfort and uneasiness, so much so that she'd avoided him as much as possible since coming home from the hospital. The idea of spending any amount of time with him made her skin crawl with pure dread. But he was right. If there was one chance in a million that he was the father of her baby, then he deserved an opportunity to tell her about the relationship they had shared before her accident. A relationship that might have produced her child.

Chapter Eight

"Say ahhh."

Jenny opened her mouth wide and complied with Doc Porter's request. When he was finished peering down her throat, she asked, "Why do doctors always say that?"

Doc chuckled. "We don't mean to be annoying." He gently pressed on the glands in her neck. Absently, he continued his explanation, "Making the sound tenses the tongue, gives a better view of the tonsils. Yours look good, by the way."

He shined a light first in one eye, then the other, checking her pupil reflexes.

"Any headaches?" he asked.

She shook her head negatively. "I feel great."

"Good." He felt her neck again. "Very good."

"Physically, anyway," she added softly.

He leaned back against the cabinets, crossing his arms, and dipped his chin so he could look at her over his bifocals. "I heard you and Luke were working things out."

Jenny's brows raised. "And here I thought life was

pretty isolated up there on that mountain. News travels fast in Olem.''

Doc shrugged. ''Not really. I talked to Mary.''

''Oh.''

''Does that bother you? That Mary and I talked?'' he asked. ''You're more than just my patient, you know. And Mary's your friend. We care about you.''

''It doesn't bother me. In fact, I kind of like the idea that people are watching out for me.'' She smiled at him. ''It's just that, with everyone watching and talking—'' she grinned ''—it's impossible to hide anything.''

''Oh, you can hide plenty if you've a mind to.''

The rejoinder was meant with no malice intended, Jenny knew. Doc had simply wanted to add a little something to her teasing quip. But his statement wiped the smile right off her face.

''Doc,'' she said, her tone turning serious, ''was I the kind of person who hid things?''

Before he could answer, other questions rolled from her lips. ''Was I the kind of woman who would have an affair right under her husband's nose? Is it really possible that I'd sleep with Chad? Luke says no. Chad says yes. And they're both sticking to their stories—''

''Whoa.'' Doc held up a hand, palm out. ''Slow down a minute. First, let me assure you that the Jenny Prentice I knew—and still know—is kind and decent and honest.'' He reached up and toyed with his clean-shaved chin. ''As to whether or not you slept with Chad...I can't say. I *can* tell you that since Chad returned home, things have been tense. Not just in the Prentice family, either. Everyone remotely connected to the ski resort has been in wait-and-see mode.'' He shook his head, softly adding, ''Chad seems to cause ripples of strain wherever he goes, whatever he does.''

"But he couldn't have caused *that* much stress between me and Luke," Jenny said, "not if our marriage had been strong." She wished her observation has sounded more like a statement and less like a question. The uncertainty in her tone reminded her so much of her husband.

Luke had said that everything would work out. But the doubt she continued to hear in his voice, continued to read in his gaze, hurt her terribly, even though she fully understood what he was feeling and why he felt it. His thoughts, actions and words were completely justified. But she was wounded, nonetheless, and the special bond they'd found wasn't enough to transcend even the mere idea that she might have had an affair with Chad.

Thoughts of her brother-in-law brought strangely discomfiting emotions, somewhat akin to slipping her arms into a damp sweater. Jenny knew she had to let Chad have his say. That was only fair and right. But that didn't mean she had to look forward to the experience, and the dread twisting in her gut over the prospect was what had compelled her to avoid him for the past few days.

She was baffled by her attitude toward Chad. She hadn't a single memory of him, good or bad or indifferent, so why did she experience this odd darkness that bordered on creepy at the idea of spending time alone with him? Her brother-in-law had been friendly enough toward her, hadn't he? Of course, there had been that one incident in the kitchen when he'd turned on her, angrily calling her that vile name. But he'd apologized for that. Had explained his behavior in a way that made her fully understand his overwhelming frustration. Heck, they were all overwhelmed. They were all frustrated. All because of her. What she *should* be feeling for Chad was sympathy, and a generous tolerance. Not this uneasiness that was so close to fear...

An eerie shiver surged across her skin. She shook it off, sure she was being absolutely ridiculous.

"One thing you must remember—"

Doc's soft voice brought her back to the present.

"—is that we humans are fallible. We make mistakes."

"Then you think I did it," she said. "You think I made a mistake." Almost to herself, she murmured, "A terrible mistake."

"I didn't say that. I don't know if you did or you didn't." He cocked his head to one side. "The point I was trying to make was that life goes on. You need to live in the here and now. Not in what might or might not have happened in the past. Especially when you may never remember."

Jenny felt almost free behind the wheel of the Bronco on the drive back home. Sure, the worry and doubt and questions were still there, strong as ever, but out here on the open road, shoving her troubles behind her was easy and she simply enjoyed the sunshine and the broad, blue sky ahead.

Before Luke would let her drive into Olem alone, he had made her practice stopping and starting, parking and turning. With a warm smile, she remembered the hour or so they had spent driving around and around the resort parking lot. Finally, when it had been clear she was ready for the highway, but he continued to coach and lecture like a worried mother hen, Jenny had laughed at him until he, too, was chuckling at his overprotective behavior.

Being with Luke always lightened her heart. Well, almost always, anyway. The baby, or more specifically the question of her child's paternity, was constantly between them, like a wide, turbulent river. And no matter how hard they tried to ignore it, the problem continually threatened to carry them off on its raging currents.

If only she and Luke could take Doc's advice and forget whatever had been in the past and live for today. But somehow Jenny couldn't see either one of them doing that.

Driving around to the back of the house, Jenny parked and then hurried to the kitchen door. Mary was sure to need help fixing dinner.

But the kitchen was empty when she pushed open the door.

"Mary?"

No pots were simmering on the stove. No rich aromas wafting in the air. The room, the whole house, had a lonely, deserted feel.

Wondering what could have happened to Mary, Jenny automatically crossed the room and picked up the phone. She realized she didn't have the slightest idea what Mary's telephone number was, so she pulled open the drawer and took out the small address book, the one with the cute puppies on the cover.

Her index finger was poised on the number when Chad entered the kitchen.

"Hi."

His charming smile was a bit disarming, but not enough to take her mind off the task at hand.

"Have you heard from Mary?" Jenny asked him. "I'm a little worried. She should be here."

"She was here," Chad said. "I sent her home."

"Oh." She blinked, that odd disquiet sprouting to life inside her. "But why? Luke likes her to be here with me in the afternoons."

Chad shrugged, his smile showing more white teeth.

"I'll be here with you this afternoon. I'll even help you with dinner."

"B-but," she stammered, "doesn't Luke need you up on the mountain? Clearing the new trails?"

His expression changed right before her eyes. The vibrations emanating off him were filled with a sudden disdain.

"I think Mr. Fully Capable will be just fine without me. In fact, he'd probably prefer that I wasn't up there getting in the way."

She didn't like his sarcastic tone. "I'm sure Luke doesn't feel that way."

His mouth twisted derisively, and Jenny wondered whether Chad wasn't aware that his emotions were showing so openly, or if the man simply didn't care.

"He does his best to tolerate my incompetence without remarking on it too awful much." He breathed a sympathy-garnering sigh.

Annoyance flared up inside her. Jenny had never heard Luke say one word against his brother. However, her irritation petered out when she realized that she, too, had come to the conclusion that Luke was barely tolerating Chad's presence at the resort. If Chad had noticed it, then it was no wonder he felt resentful and self-pitying.

Feeling the need to say something supportive, she remarked, "You're being too hard both on yourself and on Luke, don't you think?"

Another careless shrug. "Maybe. Maybe not."

Silence settled over them. The air around them seemed to grow tense, strained.

Jenny's gaze darted to the digital clock on the stove. Luke wouldn't be home for hours yet. That was a lot of awkward time to fill.

She pulled open the door of one of the lower cabinets.

"I guess I could start dinner," she said, reaching for a pot.

"It's too early for that."

Her hand stilled for a moment, and then she drew it back and closed the door. "You're probably right. Mary and I often sit and have a cup of tea and a good gossip session before we start cooking."

The uneasy atmosphere seemed to swell almost painfully, like a badly bruised knee or a battered arm.

"You've been avoiding me lately," he said.

She didn't even try to deny it. Her voice was soft as she answered, "Yes."

He looked hurt as he remarked, "I couldn't help but notice that you *haven't* been avoiding my brother."

"Luke is my husband," she pointed out, striving for a firmness that might circumvent the unpleasant argument she felt brewing.

"And I'm your lover."

His bluntness caught her off guard. She gasped.

"I, uh, well…but…" She stopped and took a moment to sort her thoughts. "But, Chad, you know I don't remember that. What we may have had, I mean."

"What we *may* have had?"

The glint of aggression in his brown eyes sparked a tiny flash of fear in her. "Look," she said, "I don't want to fight with you. If you're going to argue and accuse, then we'll have to do this some other time. Some other place."

When Luke is within shouting distance, came a silent cry.

His brow creased with what she took to be bewilderment.

"You're not afraid of me, are you?" he asked.

"No." She was unable to believe she stared at him so boldly as she lied.

"Good." His voice softened with another smile. "Because that's the last thing I'd want." After a moment, he said, "You have to understand why I'm upset. You do, don't you? It's just that you and I, we had something wonderful. So wonderful that we made a child. Our child. And I feel like I'm losing you. And our baby. To Luke."

The reproach pulsing off him made her feel the need to explain.

"Ever since the accident," she began, "I've felt like my entire life is some gigantic jigsaw puzzle that's been dropped, the pieces scattered in every direction. I've been spending time with Luke trying to gather some of those pieces together."

He nodded slowly, censure written clearly on his face. "I could understand that, but does the process have to include holding hands and kissing?"

Pressing her lips together, she averted her gaze.

"I feel betrayed."

His blunt honesty made her knees go weak with shame.

"I can see how you'd feel hurt," she said. "If you and I had been having an affair—"

"*If.*" The small word grated harshly. "There you go again, talking like you don't believe you and I were lovers."

She wanted to cringe at his bold description of their relationship. What could possibly have happened between her and Luke that might have pushed her into her brother-in-law's arms? Her husband had admitted they'd had problems, but he'd put her off when she'd asked about them. Did she dare query Chad on the subject?

"Come into the living room," Chad said. "I have something I want to show you."

She followed him out into the hallway, past the staircase and into the formal living room. Chad settled onto the couch and patted the spot next to him. Jenny hesitantly eased herself down beside him, leaving several inches of cushion between them.

Reaching toward the coffee table, he picked up a dusty album and slid it onto her lap.

"Here," he said, sudden excitement lighting his brown eyes. "I think it's time you saw this."

"What's in it?" But she was opening the mottled blue cover as she asked, feeling all the while as if she was about to receive some dreadful news.

"You'll see," was all Chad would say.

The nervous energy radiating from him had her feeling tense and on her guard. The photo album's spine crackled as she spread the cover wide on her lap.

She recognized her own smiling face in the pictures, as well as Chad's, but the other faces were strangers to her, and by that she really wasn't surprised. There was a great deal of fun and partying in the images. Lots of smiles, lots of camaraderie. And many, many beer bottles.

There were pictures that had been taken at a college football game. She read Go Wildcats on a banner, Villanova on another. Some of the photos had been taken in what were obviously messy college dorm rooms. There were pictures snapped at the ski resort, too. The mountains looked so different covered with snow. One thing Jenny did notice was that Luke was not in even one of the pictures in the album.

"That's a hefty piece of your puzzle, don't you think?" Chad asked. "Did Luke tell you about that?"

The tone of his question irked her. It was as though he was certain Luke had been less than honest with her.

"He told me all about it." She was relieved and actually happy to be able to say that. "He told me you and I attended Villanova together. He also told me that he and I met when you brought your college friends to the resort during the ski season."

Chad leaned forward, inching closer to her, his voice soft and deadly serious as he asked, "Did he tell you that you and I dated all through college?"

The room seemed to tip. Very slowly. Very methodically. And Jenny eased her hand out and grasped the plush, padded armrest of the couch so she wouldn't topple over when the world went too far off-kilter.

She couldn't have heard Chad correctly. She simply couldn't have. And if she had heard him accurately, then the story just couldn't be true. Because Luke surely would have told her about something this momentous, something this vital to the situation they all found themselves in. Wouldn't he?

Several reasons why he might choose not to tell her came rushing at her. But she deflected them as best she could, feeling the need to keep her wits firmly in check.

Forcing a calming inhalation into her lungs, Jenny told herself not to panic, determined not to slide off into hysterical oblivion. She would simply treat this information as just one more piece to the puzzle.

"You're serious." Her throat felt raspy, but she was determined to go on. "You're not lying to me, are you?"

"Cross my heart." Chad made a small X high on the left side of his chest. "I wouldn't lie to you, Jenny."

The smile that sauntered its way onto his mouth looked so sincere that she found it unnerving. She pressed trembling fingers to her lips, her mind whirling.

If she and Chad had dated in college, if the two of them had been an "item" when she had come to Prentice Mountain to ski, then why hadn't Luke told her? And since he hadn't, didn't that mean he had not been truthful, just as Chad had suggested with his sarcasm? The wall of trust she'd built with her husband began to wobble, to and fro.

"Tell me—" Hearing the weakness in her tone and hating it, she stopped, cleared her throat and started again. "Tell me about us."

An eerie wave washed over her as she remembered making the same request of Luke. She bit her lip to keep her chin from quivering. She didn't like this discovery. She didn't like the idea that her husband had been choosy about the things he'd revealed to her.

"We were so good together, you and I," Chad said.

Inching closer, he reached out and took her hand. Jenny was too numb, too drained to resist.

"The two of us were inseparable." The pad of his thumb made small, dry circles on her knuckle. "All our friends teased us. They would laugh and say that we were joined at the hip. Because neither of us would do anything, go anywhere, unless our other half was present." His laugh was lighthearted as he added, "It was like we were married."

"It was?" Shock and disbelief made her sound far off, distant.

"Yeah," he told her easily. "We were like this." He lifted one hand, crossing his index and middle fingers in a tight, intimate embrace.

Her lips went bone-dry and she moistened them with her tongue. "If we were so close, what happened? Why didn't we end up together? You know, why didn't we get married?"

His hand dropped, clamping onto hers, and his eyes grew hard. "Because my older brother stole you away from me, that's why. You belonged to me, and he took you when my back was turned.''

Bitterness poured from him, hot, sharp and heavy. A festering venom that spurted from his eyes, his voice, and even seemed to seep from the tips of his fingers as he touched her skin.

''He'll do anything,'' Chad continued, ''say anything to get you to stay with him. He did before your accident. He will now, too. You'll have to be very careful. I know my brother. He can be vicious when he wants to be.''

The person Chad described didn't sound at all like the Luke Jenny had come to know, the Luke she'd come to care for. And there was something that felt *twisted* about the scenario Chad had described, something about his description of the past that simply didn't seem right. But for the life of her, she couldn't decide what it might be.

With no warning, Chad slid his fingers over her cheek, cradling her jaw in his palm. Jenny's initial urge was to pull away, but the pleading in his eyes, like the hypnotic flute of a cobra trainer, held her entranced.

''Promise me you'll be careful,'' he whispered softly, earnest concern etched in his face. ''Promise me you won't just believe everything he says. Come to me. We'll talk about anything you want. Anything he tells you.''

Anxiety and a rush of panicky adrenaline shot through her system, making her heart pound, her ears buzz. Who was telling the truth? Who should she believe?

Evidently, Chad recognized exactly what she was thinking.

''It's okay,'' he crooned. ''It's really okay.'' His hand trailed down to the curve of her neck, where it settled.

Only half-aware of the gentle kneading of his fingers, Jenny focused on his soothing voice. Her head felt so fogged with confusion.

"I'm not asking you to believe my story over his," he said. "All I want is for you to give me a fair shot. Don't believe him over me. Not without giving me a chance to explain whatever he might come up with." He moistened his bottom lip. "What kind of mean things has Luke been saying about me?"

She took a moment to think, to concentrate on his question, and then gave a tiny shake of her head.

"Oh, come on now," he coaxed, his fingers trailing to the back of her neck. "I can't believe my brother hasn't taken every opportunity to demean my character."

"Really," she told him, the sudden urge to defend her husband seeming to come out of nowhere, "he hasn't."

Chad looked dubious, but didn't push her further, and for that she was grateful. The bewildered haze clogging her brain had her feeling flustered, slow-witted, and her thoughts seemed to be crawling like molasses.

She blinked, becoming sluggishly aware of how close Chad was. One of his hands caressed her neck, the other was planted intimately on her thigh. And she was sitting there on the couch, docile as a lamb.

Her eyes widened. He was leaning toward her, his intention of kissing her crystal clear.

"Wait," she said, suddenly frantic to escape. But his hand on her neck made any retreat impossible.

Knee-jerk instinct had her reaching up, pressing her fingertips against his lips. She wasn't able to push him away, but she did stall his forward momentum.

"I'm not ready for this," she told him.

You'll never be ready for this, her subconscious told her.

The ardor lighting his chocolate eyes didn't dim one iota as he took her hand in his, turned it and kissed her knuckles. "How do you know?" he asked. "Were you ready for Luke's kisses?"

"That's none of your business." But she was sure her eagerness to be kissed by her husband was exposed in the flaming hue of her face.

Chad's query was much too personal for comfort. He had no right asking her such a question. Yet she was relieved that the chaste, cheek-kiss exchange between herself and Luke had been *all* Chad had seen. The memory of her husband's heated mouth on hers on a couple of other occasions caused a stirring of hunger in her even now. And that craving made Chad's closeness, the feel of his cool, dry lips on her fingers, almost repulsive.

Pulling her hand from his grasp, she said, "I don't want to do this, Chad. It doesn't feel right."

His other hand was still firmly anchored on the back of her neck. He didn't hurt her, but he didn't release her, either.

"It used to feel good," he whispered, his breath brushing her cheek. "It used to feel right."

She searched his eyes. "I don't care if it felt right. If we had an affair, it was wrong. *We* were wrong."

"We were in love," he insisted. "And if anyone was wrong, it was Luke. He shouldn't have stolen my woman."

"That's the second time you've referred to me as if I were your possession."

His gaze clouded with sudden passion, his fingers on her nape tightening perceptively. "You used to like it. Back in college, you *wanted* me to call you 'my woman.' You wanted that desperately."

Fear rumbled through her like an earth tremor. Placing the flat of her hand on his chest, she said, her voice tight, "Please let go of me, Chad."

Something in her tone made him lean back an inch. He blinked, his face going slack with surprise.

"You're afraid of me." He frowned. And then his expression grew wounded.

Frightening her had evidently not been his aim; however, the insistence in his words, the intensity in his gaze had been too much for her. But now, seeing that the fear she'd revealed had hurt him, she felt something akin to shame to know that she'd misread his intentions.

She felt sorry for Chad. Sorry that he so obviously felt deeply about her. Sorry that he wanted so much for her to remember what they had shared. She felt sorry about this whole situation.

"Don't be afraid of me, Jenny," he said.

He looked absolutely wretched, and pity welled up inside her.

She dropped her hand from his chest. "Oh, Chad," she said. "I'm sorry. Don't be hurt." She sighed. "You have to remember, I have no memory of what we had. Back in college. Or even two weeks ago. You have to be patient. Just like I have to be patient. Emotions can't be forced."

Reaching up, he captured her chin between his fingers. "It's so hard to be patient when I *do* remember what we had. How you felt about me. How you needed me." He chuckled, his voice turning husky as he added, "How you pursued me. And I miss it. I miss it terribly."

His brash intimation didn't really have time to sink in before she realized he was leaning toward her, desire etched once again in his cinnamon eyes.

"Don't," she insisted, planting her hand firmly on his chest again. "I don't want to do this."

His body stilled and he dismissed her wishes with a slight roll of his eyes. "How do you know you don't want to," he said, sensuous suggestion oozing from every word, "if you don't try it?" He gifted her with a languorous, sexy smile. "You might discover that you *do* want to do this. I know *I* do."

But I don't feel anything for you, she wanted to shout. *Not anything close to the attraction I feel for Luke.*

"You certainly enjoyed kissing me before," he told her. "You enjoyed doing lots of things with me."

His suggestion made her nauseous.

With a gentle pressure on her neck, he pulled her to him.

"No." Her tone was firmer now.

Again he looked hurt, and again she felt pity. But sympathy was not a good motivation for giving in to his ardent demand.

Pushing him back, she slipped from under his arm. She saw the photo album that had somehow found its way onto the coffee table, and she picked it up, hugging it to her chest like a shield.

Awkwardness stiffened the air, making it moist, sticky, uncomfortable. There was Chad sitting on the couch so obviously wanting her, and here she stood, repulsed by the mere idea of his kiss. Jenny didn't want to hurt his feelings, but she had to make him understand how she felt.

"It isn't a good idea for us to be getting…physical," she said. "I appreciate your talking to me. For showing me the pictures. For filling in some more of the pieces of my past—"

"*Our* past," he corrected.

"Yes, well…" The rest of the thought faded. She inhaled deeply, feeling truly overwhelmed. "If you don't mind, I'd like to go lie down for awhile. You've given me a lot to think about."

She backed up several slow steps, overcome by a strange reluctance to turn her back on him.

"Don't worry about cooking," he told her, his voice sugary-sweet. "I'll have pizza delivered."

Jenny nodded vaguely, her thoughts a jumbled, chaotic whirl, but as she spun on her heel and rushed from the room, dinner was the last thing on her mind.

Chapter Nine

Afternoon sunlight streamed through the soft sheers that covered her bedroom windows. Up until this moment, this room had been a calming sanctuary, but now Jenny didn't even see its muted, serene colors, couldn't capture even one minute molecule of tranquility in the heavy air.

Her blood churned too quickly, causing her ears to whoosh with each and every frantic heartbeat. Questions flooded her brain like the churning waters of a rain-swollen river. Frenzied. Incessant.

Why hadn't Luke been completely honest with her? Why hadn't he told her that she and Chad had dated? That was such a profound piece of information. Was it true that Luke had edged his way into her heart years ago, when she'd still been in love with Chad? *Had* he stolen her away from his brother? And if that was true, why would she have let such a thing happen?

She tossed the photo album onto the bed and rubbed her fingers over her face. She felt tired. Weary of all these questions. Exhausted from having gone day after day without knowing the honest truth. The full truth.

Heaving a sigh, she couldn't help but feel that there was something...*off* about Chad's story. Some small part that didn't ring true. But she wasn't able to decipher why she felt that way. Oh, she was certain he was telling the truth about their having dated in college. She glanced at the album. Proof. There was no getting around the undeniable proof of those snapshots.

However, even with all the new pieces of the puzzle her brother-in-law had handed her, she still wasn't able to view the entire picture. There were still things she didn't know. Things she hadn't been told. Like what had happened to cause Luke to stop sharing the master suite with her? Why had he moved his things to his office downstairs? And what had Doc meant today when he'd said that Chad's return to the mountain had everyone connected with the resort feeling tense and waiting? What was everyone anticipating? Surely everyone knew about her previous relationship with her brother-in-law. Her face flamed as she imagined them all—Mary, Bud, Doc, and a hundred or so other people she hadn't even met yet—expectant and watchful, knowing she would betray Luke now that Chad had returned to Prentice Mountain.

Suddenly she felt as though she were riding a maniacal merry-go-round, the music eerie and loud, the huge, dark horses leering, laughing at her as they bounced up and down, up and down, faster and faster, refusing to let her get off.

Fleeing from the room, she slipped down the stairs, out the front door and allowed herself to be swallowed up by the thick pine forest.

"Jenny!"

Luke had called until his throat was raw. The sun was

setting. Where could she be? The Bronco was in the garage. Chad's car was parked in the drive. She certainly couldn't have walked into Olem. The town was miles and miles away. Even Bud and Mary lived nearly four miles from the resort. A trek to their house was at least feasible. However, when he'd called there an hour ago, he'd been told that Jenny hadn't been seen or heard from.

He and Chad had argued when he'd come home from work. It seemed there wasn't a pleasant word to be had between him and his brother these days. He didn't guess there would be, as long as Jenny's affections were still up for grabs. Luke wanted more than anything to mend his relationship with his wife. Until he did, he didn't really have any right to tell Chad to keep away from her.

Especially when his brother might be the father of the baby she carried, a tiny voice echoed through his mind.

Hell, he refused to believe it. He just plain refused.

The photo album he'd found on her bed told him she knew about her prior relationship with his brother when she was in college. He should have told her. He knew that. But he hadn't, for the simple reason of wanting to get closer to her first.

Calling her name again, he shoved aside the thick undergrowth and made his way toward the creek. He hadn't yet looked there for her.

The idea that Jenny's baby might be Chad's floated once again through his brain, as it had hundreds of times over the past weeks. Angrily, he slammed shut the door on the thought.

It couldn't be true.

His hands balled into fists as doubt seeped into his mind. Why had he pushed her away from him all those weeks ago? he silently railed at himself. Why had he allowed his own fears and insecurities to get the best of him? Why hadn't he laid bare the secret he'd kept from her since their marriage? As it was, his stubborn determination to hide what he'd done all those years ago might have been the catalyst that had pushed her into Chad's arms. Into Chad's bed.

No! he told himself. His wife hadn't slept with his brother.

Chad said she had. The words grated against Luke's brain.

"Chad says a lot of things," he muttered.

However, Jenny wasn't in a position to refute his brother's claim. And that was what tore at Luke's heart, ripping it to shreds.

Where in the name of heaven could she be?

As if his guardian angel suddenly decided to bestow the gift of an answer, he saw her. She was sleeping on a soft bed of fragrant pine needles, the trickling creek singing its unending song not two feet from her head. The relief that swamped him was dizzying in its intensity.

Not wanting to frighten her, he approached quietly.

"Jenny." He took another tentative step toward her. "Wake up, honey. It's time to go home."

Her eyes fluttered open. The soft brown eyes of an innocent doe. Gorgeous. Luke felt his blood quicken.

Sighing and rolling onto her back, she gave him a sleepy smile.

"Hi," he said, stifling his urge to march up to her and demand to know why she wanted to scare the living daylights out of him by running off without a word.

She sat up, looking disoriented and disheveled with needles and a tiny pinecone tangled in her silky golden hair. Luke thought she'd never looked lovelier.

Again she sighed. "What time is it?" she asked, her voice husky with sleep.

She combed her fingers through her shoulder-length tresses and the pinecone fell to the ground.

"It's way past dinner," he told her. "Are you hungry? There's plenty of pizza left."

Jenny blinked at his mention of food as if it brought something to her mind, something that the imprisoning sleep-fogged haze had caused her to forget until just this moment.

She pushed herself to her feet, absently brushing pine needles and dirt from her cute little denim-clad butt in a manner Luke found sexy as hell.

"You lied to me," she said, looking him directly in the eye.

She plunked her hands on her hips. She was trying to evince a tremendous amount of anger and indignation, but the fact that she'd just awakened from a deep sleep was working against her. Luke could see that. Her movements were slow, her face soft. The look she gave him couldn't quite be called a glare, but it was close enough.

"Why didn't you tell me that Chad and I dated?" she asked. "Why didn't you tell me how close he and I were before you and I got together?"

"I didn't lie to you, Jenny."

"You don't think you're guilty by omission?"

Inhaling deeply, he nodded. "Probably. But it was only because—"

"Don't," she cut him off. "Don't explain. Don't say another word. I can't tell you how sick I am of hearing half truths and innuendoes and brother bad-mouthing brother."

He clamped his lips shut. He might not have fully explained things a time or two, but only because he'd thought it was best for her. For *them*. However, he'd never made even one derogatory insinuation regarding the situation they found themselves in, and he worked hard at not casting any aspersions on his brother's character, no matter how much he might want to. So Luke guessed Jenny's last two complaints were transgressions his brother had committed.

Still, he remained silent. He couldn't concern himself with Chad's wrongdoing, not when his own sins were quickly catching up with him.

With a jerky motion, Jenny tucked a strand of hair behind her ear. She'd wanted so desperately to trust Luke. Had put her faith in him. Had allowed the desire she felt for him to flourish and grow until it enveloped and saturated her thoughts, her dreams.

However, now that she'd discovered he'd only told her bits and pieces of the truth, she couldn't help but wonder if he was worthy of her trust. She felt she was on some huge see-saw, teetering back and forth, up and down, as she pondered who to believe and what the real truth was.

"Since the day I woke up in the hospital," she said, "I've been trying to piece together my past. I find a sliver here, and a sliver there. And some of them are like sharp shards of glass. They cut. They draw blood."

Luke was looking at her like he had no idea where this tangent of hers was leading. Well, that was fine, because neither did she.

"He said you stole me away from him," she said. "He called me his *property*." Embarrassment forced her to avert her gaze. Her voice grew faint as she mused, "What kind of woman was I that I would have allowed myself to be thought of in that manner?"

She was terribly afraid of the answer to that question

and she prayed her husband wouldn't respond. She rushed to say, "He said *I* was the one who did the pursuing. Chad talked about my relationship with him in a blatantly sexual way." A shiver coursed through her as she remembered it. "It made me so...uncomfortable."

As if a light had snapped on in her mind, she suddenly realized what she was saying and who she was saying it to. Her gaze widened as it flew to Luke's face. She took in his handsome features, strained and paled by what he'd been hearing. Some fearfully painful emotion flickered in his beautiful ebony eyes, and Jenny was horrified, knowing that she was responsible for it being there.

She pressed both hands, one atop the other, to the base of her throat. "Oh, Luke, I'm so sorry. You're the last person I should be telling this to."

He remained still and silent, and as they stood there in the forest, Jenny remembered something he'd told her days ago. He'd said that Chad hadn't known about her marriage until his return to Prentice Mountain a few short months ago. He'd said Chad had been gone, without a letter or phone call, for nearly five years. Yet Chad had said that Luke had stolen her from him.

"Let me ask you something," she blurted. "Did you and I get together before Chad left for Europe? Or after?"

"After," he said. "I didn't approach you with any personal relationship in mind until my brother was completely out of the picture."

There it was again, she noticed. That feeling that something was just a little off. Like sheets of wallpaper, the two designs were the same, but the pattern didn't quite match at the seams.

Questions tugged at her again. But these questions involved her relationship with Chad, and some of the things he'd told her, things that somehow didn't seem to ring true. She was anxious for some answers—answers that only her brother-in-law could give her.

"I have to go talk to Chad," she said.

"But—"

The bewilderment in Luke's tone made her lift her gaze to his, her impatience to be off expressed in her eyes.

"I think we should talk," he told her. "What about your accusation that I was guilty of lying by omission?"

He looked so befuddled to realize she was no longer focusing her anger on him that she nearly smiled. But she didn't dare.

"I want to explain."

The candor in his black eyes nearly made her veer off course.

"And I want to hear every word of your explanation," she told him. "I also think it's high time you told me why you moved out of our bedroom." She paused for only a fraction of a second. "But right now, I have to speak to Chad. I think I just may have caught him in a big, fat lie. And if I have, then I think it's his responsibility to answer to that."

With purposeful strides, she headed toward home.

When she came into the house through the kitchen door, she saw Chad sitting at the table munching on the crust of the last slice of pizza.

"Luke's out looking for you," he said.

She nodded. "He found me."

"The man does overreact." Chad chuckled. "He wanted to call out Olem's Search and Rescue team. And he would have too, it I hadn't told him that was going a bit overboard."

"Thanks for keeping your head." There was a testiness in her tone that Chad didn't seem to notice. She hadn't been aware that she'd caused Luke to worry and felt instantly contrite that she had. The fact that he'd gone looking for her was just one more example of his sweet, caring nature.

Her gaze landed on the empty pizza box sitting on the tabletop.

Chad wiped his mouth on a napkin and tossed it in the box. "I got kind of hungry while I was waiting for Luke to get back. I didn't think you'd mind, since it was getting too late for you to eat dinner, anyway."

She didn't even bother trying to figure out his strange logic. All she knew was that being in his presence was an enlightening experience—one that taught her a lot about his character. Maybe that was why Luke had suggested she spend time with him.

"I'd like to talk," she told him.

"Sure."

He started to stand, but she stopped him.

"Just sit there," she said, feeling a sudden panic that he might actually touch her again.

"What is it?" he asked. "You seem upset."

"Tell me why you went away to Europe," she said. "Tell me why you left me here."

"Luke complained to you about the money, didn't he? I just knew he would."

There was such venom in his words, Jenny felt the urge to step back, but she repressed it.

"What money?" The query flowed off her tongue before she had time to think. "Luke didn't say anything about any money. I don't know what you're talking about."

"Sure, he didn't," Chad spat out. "And I'm the tooth fairy. I know my brother, and this is just his style. To use something like this against me. He's been jealous of my trip for years.''

Jenny watched his jaw tense.

''I deserved that money,'' he went on. ''It was my inheritance, to do whatever I wanted with. Dad took a loan against the resort so I could have the trip of a lifetime. I deserved that money. I deserved that experience. And I refuse to feel guilty because Luke is bitter about it.''

The information Chad was giving her hadn't been at all what she'd expected. But the more he talked, the more he revealed. Not about his relationship with her, but about his relationship with Luke.

''So, you didn't work your way across Europe?'' she asked.

She had no idea why she'd assumed he had taken jobs to support himself on his travels, but when Luke had told her that Chad had gone off to see the world, that's exactly what she had thought.

''Of course not.'' He looked appalled by the suggestion. ''What fun would that have been?''

For *five years* he'd traveled from country to country on money his father had given him? Money that had been borrowed against the resort?

And Luke stayed behind to run the business, pay off the debt, care for their father when he took sick, bury him when he died. No wonder he felt bitter and resentful toward his brother, even though she'd seen how he tried to hide those feelings, beating himself up for feeling them. Now she understood that Luke might have been right when he'd suggested his father had overindulged his youngest son.

Sadness washed over her as she realized that Chad didn't really care how his actions affected those around him. All he cared about was procuring his own selfish

desires. The empty pizza box and his odd reasoning behind why he should be the one to eat the last slice was
simple proof of this theory.

"Chad, I honestly didn't know anything about how you
supported yourself when you went abroad," she told him.
"What I wanted to know had to do strictly with you and
me. I wanted to know why you left if we were as close
as you told me we were."

The anger he'd expressed only a moment before
seemed to dissolve and his brown eyes narrowed warily.

"You didn't write, or call, or visit," she said, working
hard to keep accusation from her voice. If she was going
to get answers from him, she had to keep the conversation
as nonthreatening as possible.

She leaned her back against the corner of the doorjamb.
"Had we made some kind of pact?" she asked. "Was I
supposed to wait for you? Or what?" She lifted on shoulder. "What was your plan?"

"W-well," he stammered, "you were going to wait for
me. You promised to, anyway."

This last statement was said with a large measure of
reproach.

"But you were gone for *years*," she pointed out. "You
honestly expected me to wait when you didn't bother to
contact me?"

She watched his eyes shift as he tried to come up with
something to say. Before he could regroup, she hit him
with, "Did we part on good terms, Chad?"

The idea that she'd confront him with these questions
had obviously never entered his head. Jenny guessed he'd
thought she'd simply believe whatever it was he chose to
tell her. The sheer arrogance of that kind of attitude an-
gered her. Chad's reactions to her questions, coupled with
the fact that his account of the situation didn't add up,

made it clear that he was lying. Luke might have given her half truths, but at least what he'd told her had been fact.

"When you told me that Luke had stolen me away from you—" she hated speaking about herself as if she was a possession to be owned by one or the other of the Prentice brothers "—I assumed that you'd left the mountain because you were hurt by my relationship with Luke. That seeing the two of us together was too upsetting for you. However, you described your trip as, quote, 'a chance of a lifetime,' and something you deserved. This trip wasn't a whim. It wasn't an escape." Her tone had become more and more accusatory with each sentence. "It had to have been planned. Obtaining a loan on the resort had to take your father some time, what with applications and appraisals and all that red tape. And Luke and I didn't get together, in any personal way at least, until after you'd left."

She felt fully confident in adding this last piece of information provided by Luke.

I deserved that money, Chad's words reverberated in her head. *I deserved that experience.*

Those two declarations pretty much summed up the Chad Jenny had come to know over the past weeks. He felt he was entitled to all the good things life had to offer with none of the hard work. Like a fantasy trip across Europe that was paid for by the sweat of his poor father's brow. Chad was the type of person who would sit down in a room full of people and abruptly change the conversation because he'd never, for a moment, believe that every single person present wouldn't be dying to hear what he had to say. He was the kind of person who ate the last slice of pizza.

Jenny remembered the conversation she'd had with her

husband about Chad. Luke had expressed anger at himself over his inability to erase the negative emotions he felt toward his brother. She hadn't really understood what he was going through. Until now.

Nodding to herself, she realized that now she probably had a clearer comprehension of his feelings than he had himself.

"I just realized something, Chad," she said. "I don't like you." She crossed her arms over her chest, amazed that she didn't feel the least bit anxious or fearful about delivering the news.

Chad laughed. His disbelieving chuckle fanned the flames of her hostility.

"You don't mean that," he told her. "You don't know what you're saying."

"Oh, but I know exactly what I'm saying." Leaning her shoulder against the doorjamb, she continued, "You bring out some strong feelings in me. From the moment I woke up in the hospital, I felt fearful of you. I don't know why. I may never know why. But you unsettle me. Make me feel awkward and uncomfortable."

Her brother-in-law's eyes lit up with what looked to be a challenge.

"There was a time," he said, "not too long ago, when I made you feel *other* things."

The lewdness in his voice turned her stomach.

"You said that before." Her anger flared hotter. "I don't understand the necessity for your filthy tone. I get the feeling you think that's going to turn me on, or something. Well, it doesn't. It achieves just the opposite, in fact. I find your obscene suggestions offensive."

Her arm muscles grew taut and she hugged herself even tighter. "There *may* have been a time when I felt something sexual for you. But I can assure you, if that's true, I was a different person then. A very different person.''

The arrogance and self-assurance slowly drained from his face, and Jenny got the impression that he was just getting the first hint that he might not come out of this conversation smelling like a rose.

Finally, she said, ''Just so there's no misunderstanding between us, you need to know that I don't want to have anything whatsoever to do with you. You're a manipulator. You use everything possible to get your way, whether it be bullying people or tugging at their sympathies. I don't trust you. And I'd like it very much if you stayed away from me.''

Chad was stunned. ''But what about our child? I want to be a part of my baby's life.''

She understood his concern, *if* indeed he was her child's father, but Jenny was surprised that he didn't seem more upset that she'd just come out and told him there was no future for them as a couple.

Sliding a protective hand over her tummy, she said, ''There's plenty of time to worry about that. Once the baby's born, there are tests that can be run.''

''Those tests aren't accurate!''

He fairly exploded out of his chair, and Jenny reacted with a start.

''Of course they're accurate,'' she said. ''Lawsuits are settled on paternity tests every day.''

Chad glowered. ''You'd better rethink this. You and I had an affair. If you go trying to disprove that, then you'll be making a big mistake.''

Cold claws of fear grabbed her around the throat, but she refused to allow him to witness that. ''I don't like the threat I hear in your voice.'' Then his words sank in, and the fear he'd infused in her thinned and then melted away altogether. "Chad, the test can't prove we didn't have an affair," she said. "It can only prove the paternity of—"

"Look," he said, intimidation in every jab of his finger in the air. "I'm the father of that baby. And I won't allow some scientist in a lab to tell me otherwise."

The back screen door opened behind her, and Luke entered the kitchen. The ominous aura surrounding him was unmistakable.

"I think you'd better calm down, baby brother," he advised quietly.

Chad's gaze narrowed. "Don't you tell me—"

"Stop!" she said. Both men turned their gazes on her. "No more fighting. No more arguments. *No more.*"

The silence was filled with roiling emotion.

"So," her brother-in-law said, "you're choosing being with him over being with me."

She took a moment to inhale, then she shook her head. Looking Chad square in the face, she told him, "What I'm choosing is *not* to be with you."

Turning on her heel, Jenny walked out the back door, her body trembling so badly she felt sure she'd fall on her face.

Chapter Ten

Her muscles trembled with elation the likes of which Jenny had never felt before. She tipped up her chin and stared at the beautiful salmon-tinted sky. The truth of it was that she *had* felt elation this strong before. In Luke's arms.

But the joy that had her soul singing had nothing to do with her husband. The euphoria dancing inside her, making her knees weak, had everything to do with *finally* feeling free.

Ever since coming home from the hospital, Jenny had felt this tremendous pressure to make some sort of decision regarding the father of her baby. The burden of having to choose one Prentice brother over the other had been overwhelming at times.

But standing there talking to Chad, uncovering his true character, she was hit with the notion that she didn't necessarily have to live the rest of her life with either man simply because he may or may not have fathered her child. She'd realized she'd been living each day with an oppressive, albeit subconscious, idea that she had to figure out who was the true father of her baby and then make that man the center point in her life.

That subliminal message had been one of the things, she was sure, that had her feeling confused and censured about her strong physical attraction to Luke. She grinned. But it certainly hadn't been powerful enough to keep her from acting on her feelings a time or two over the past weeks.

Rounding the corner of the garage, Jenny headed for the stand of tall trees just ahead. Earlier this evening, she'd used the mountain forest to hide, from the past Chad had revealed, from the not-so-nice person he made her out to be. But now she simply wanted to enjoy the outdoors and the feeling of complete and utter freedom.

"Jenny!"

She turned and waved Luke toward her, knowing the smile she offered him held not one particle of guilt. She was through with worrying and fretting about what she should or shouldn't do, what she should or shouldn't feel, how she should or shouldn't act.

"You okay?"

The caring she heard in his voice touched her heart.

"I'm not only okay," she told him, "I feel wonderful."

Then he said, "I, ah, couldn't help but overhear the things you said to Chad."

Jenny nodded. "Good. Then I won't have to repeat to you the conversation I had with him."

She glanced toward the stand of trees, then back at him. "Chad told me you'd been out looking for me—I'm sorry to have worried you—and I know you worked all day, but can you stand a short walk? Just to the creek would be fine."

"Sure," he said, his smile tentative. "I think I can handle that."

She hadn't taken two steps before she started talking. "I've made a decision," she told him. "I've come to the conclusion that it's okay for me to lead a happy and fulfilled life, to make choices about my future based on what *I* want, and not what the old Jenny might have done, who she might have hurt." She breathed a joyous sigh. "I feel almost like I've been reborn." She glanced away. "That must sound silly to you."

"Actually, it doesn't."

Inhaling deeply, she went on, "But even though I refuse to let the past dictate my future, I still need to know about it. It's time that all the puzzle pieces were laid out on the table. I can't go another day with this fragmented picture of my life. I need to see the full image…no matter how ugly it may be. Or at least as much of it as you can show me, anyway."

The gurgle of the wide, lazy creek grew louder as they got closer. She ducked under a low-hanging branch, terribly aware that he'd made no comment whatsoever.

Leaning against a large boulder jutting up from the ground, she reached down and slipped off her shoes.

"I understand that this is going to be hard for you," she told him. "Because we're going to have to talk about my relationship with Chad."

Even in the dim twilight, she could see his eyes cloud over.

"I can't trust Chad to tell me the truth," she said. "You know that. He's too caught up in playing some kind of game. As if the man who ends up with me is the winner."

Absently tossing one shoe beside the other at the base of the rock, she said, "You knew all along Chad would lie to me, didn't you?" Her voice lowered. "That's why you kept pushing me to hear his side of the situation from him. You knew he'd lie. You knew he'd get his story tangled. And you knew I'd figure that out. Eventually.''

Luke stood only a foot or so away from her. He crossed his arms over his chest. ''It's what I hoped would happen.'' Glancing first at the ground and then back to her face, he said, ''You do understand how it would have sounded, how I would have looked, if I'd have tried to tell you…about my brother?''

''I do,'' she said softly.

Walking across the mossy ground, she glanced back over her shoulder at Luke. ''I hope you don't mind, but I've been dying to do this for days and haven't felt quite bold enough.'' Without another word, she inched her way into the cool creek.

It was shallow, only deep enough to have the water lapping at her ankles.

''The water's grand.'' She could no more stop the bubble of laughter that erupted from her throat than she could have dammed the flow of the creek.

Turning to face him, she stumbled on a small rock, gasped delightedly and lifted her arms for balance. When she looked at him, he was leaning against the boulder, one corner of his mouth cocked as he shook his head.

''What is it?'' she asked.

He took a moment to answer. Finally, he said, ''It's just that there's so much of you—'' he shrugged ''—or rather, of the old Jenny, still there. We spent many a summer night right here, with *you* right there, up to your ankles in water.''

''We did?''

He nodded.

She liked the idea of spending hot evenings here with him. Somehow it seemed fitting, right.

The forest was still, the only sound the water as it purled over and around the rocks and the high sandy places in the creek bottom. But the question that rose from the depth of her thoughts forced her to break the peaceful silence.

"When we married," she said, "did you love me?"

He uncrossed his arms, pressed his palms against the huge rock behind him. He looked to be playing for time, as if he needed to prepare his words carefully, and suddenly Jenny was afraid of what he might say.

"On the day we married," he told her, "there simply weren't words to describe how much I loved you. I never realized, until you became my wife, that I had been only half a person." His voice, his expression, his body language, seemed to intensify as he added, "You made me whole."

Shivers coursed across her skin. To be loved so completely would be a dream come true for any woman.

"Did I love you?"

"You said you did."

Something lingering in his gaze made her say, "But I didn't love you as much as you loved me?"

Chad's accusation that his brother had stolen her away rang silently in her ears.

"You can't put love on a scale, Jenny." Absently, he ran one hand over his cotton shirtfront. "I was happy with you. And I think you were happy with me."

She made her way to the edge of the creek and stepped onto the mossy bank. "Then what happened to us, Luke? Why had we separated? How come we weren't sharing a bedroom? A bed?"

His jaw tensed and he glanced into the thick treetops. For a long moment he didn't speak, didn't look at her, but Jenny was determined to wait him out.

"In order to answer that," he said, his voice sounding raw, "I'm going to have to go back to the beginning. To the very beginning, when you first started coming here to ski with Chad."

Easing herself down onto the dry, spongy ground, she sat with her legs crossed, letting him know she had all the time in the world to listen.

"You sure did hanker after Chad that first winter," he remembered softly. Then he shook his head. "But then, so did several other girls in the group." He inhaled, hesitated. "I hate to say this about my brother, but he played you all, one against the other. You were his clear favorite. However, that didn't keep him from, ah, playing the field, so to speak."

"You're kidding," she said, feeling at once offended by the idea. "But he made it sound like we were—" She cut the sentence short. "I have to keep reminding myself who and what he is."

"The winter prior to your graduation," he continued, "you gave him an ultimatum."

"Good for me," she interjected. Then she muttered, "I think."

"You wanted marriage," Luke said. "Or you were finished with him. He didn't like it. But he agreed. Dad was so excited. You'd become like a daughter to him over the past few winters. He hired you to manage the restaurant, thinking that in June you'd be moving to Prentice Mountain for good. He promised to renovate the kitchen in the summer, give you anything you'd like, and it seemed that you couldn't have been more pleased with the idea."

The way he ran his hand over his jaw revealed to her that the story was about to take a turn for the worse.

"During the following spring session, Chad came home several times without you." Absently, Luke shifted his weight on the rock, crossing one of his ankles over the other. "He started talking about a trip abroad. He said the two of you had been having trouble, and that he needed to get away. But the more he talked, the bigger this trip seemed to get. Eventually, he talked Dad out of a load of money. Chad called it 'his inheritance.' But all Dad wanted was to see Chad happy again. Dad mortgaged the resort to the gills, Chad graduated and then flew off in a 747. You arrived within the week, ready to marry Chad, ready to supervise the kitchen renovations, oblivious of my brother's departure. And his betrayal."

His voice lowered to a mere whisper as he said, "Telling you what Chad had done, that he'd gone, that I had no idea when he planned to return, was the worst thing I'd ever had to do in my life."

She watched his eyes glaze over and knew he was consumed by the memory of that moment in time when he'd delivered the bad news to her.

"You cried. You wept bitterly." He heaved a sigh. "You wouldn't let me hold you. Refused to be consoled. And then you got angry." His soft chuckle surprised her. "You cussed my brother up one side and down the other. Called him all manner of names. A couple of them even made me blush." He blinked and turned his clear, black eyes on her. "That's when I knew you'd be okay. You went to my dad. Asked him if the job was still open. Dad was happy to have you, sure that Chad would come home before too long, sure that the plans for you two to marry would go forward."

"But Chad didn't come home," she commented. "You told me that you and I got together soon after Chad left. How did your father feel about that?"

Luke lifted one shoulder a fraction. "He didn't like the idea at first. But you talked to him. Told him you loved me. That I'd make a much more stable mate. You also said Chad wouldn't be unhappy about our being together, and that you'd explain the situation to him when he came home." He grinned. "Dad fell for it, hook, line and sinker. After your talk he was completely supportive of us."

"What do you mean, 'he fell for it'?" Her tone came out sounding sharper than she'd meant. Then the bite in her words deteriorated to alarm as she asked, "Was I lying to him?"

"No, honey, no." He pushed away from the boulder, crossed the mossy ground separating them and knelt by her side, taking her hand in his. "It wasn't like that."

"So you were telling me the truth when you said he liked me?"

"Dad more than liked you," Luke told her. "He loved you. Like his own."

Her shoulders and arms sagged with relief. She couldn't understand why her relationship with her father-in-law—a man she didn't even remember—was so very important to her.

Luke's fingers curled around hers. "But Dad was never the same after Chad left."

Concern etched itself on her brow as she waited for him to elaborate.

"He became obsessed with paying off the debt," he said. "He wanted the place to be ready for Chad to take his position as a partner when he came home. Dad watched that curving lane leading up the mountain as if it was a snake about to strike. He took to drinking his morning coffee out on the front porch. And spending his last few minutes before bed out there, too.

"He wanted his baby boy to come home. Wanted him to work with the rest of us. Dad wanted Chad to be part of Prentice Ski Resort." Luke focused his dark eyes on the creek. "But Chad didn't come."

Sadness sprinkled over her like a light summer rain until she was saturated with the emotion. "I feel so sorry for your dad. For what he went through. For all that waiting. And watching."

The small smile he gave her was full of melancholy, and it was several moments before either of them spoke.

Finally, she asked, "Would it be too painful for you to tell me what happened to him?"

"Nothing sensational," he said. "He contracted bronchitis. In the dead of winter. The height of the season, no less. We were so busy, and the stubborn cuss wouldn't take care of himself. Doc ordered complete bed rest, but Dad wouldn't listen. His illness worsened until his lungs were full of pneumonia. Doc signed him into the hospital, but Dad was just too weak to pull through." He heaved a sigh. "He turned against Chad in the end. Really seemed to see his son as he is. Dad told me he was leaving the resort to me. That Chad had gotten his share of the inheritance." Luke's whole body grew heavy with sadness. "But that was only anger talking. Dad knew he was dying and was furious that he wasn't going to get a chance to see his dream come true. He did want his sons to work together. No matter how bitter he may have become in the end."

Jenny didn't know what to say. After a few minutes, she asked, "How were we?" She searched his gaze. "How did we handle your dad's death, I mean?"

"Well, we nearly ran ourselves ragged trying to care for him and keep the resort going." His thumb traced over the hills and valleys of her knuckles. "Bud and Mary were a godsend. And friends seemed to come out of the woodwork to help. And to tell the truth, Jenny, we cleaved together. Actually grew closer. I could never have survived the ordeal without you. It was hard, but we got through it. Together.''

Her heart soared to know she'd been of some help to him, even if she didn't recall having done a thing. She'd been there for him when he'd needed her. That was all that mattered to her at the moment. Then, however, a new sadness overtook her.

''If we were so close,'' she asked, ''what happened to us? I'd be an idiot not to realize that Chad's return had something to do with it. But if everything you've said about our relationship is true—'' she shook her head in bewilderment ''—how could we have let him come between us?'' She gasped as an awful idea struck her. ''Did I marry you as some sort of revenge against Chad?''

The firm, negative shake of his head relieved her anxiety.

''The separation was all my fault,'' he said, unable to look her in the face. ''You tried to talk to me about it. But I just wasn't able to bring my fears, my paranoia, out into the open.'' When his gaze found her once again, his eyes were filled with emotion laid bare. ''It was important to me that you saw me as strong, competent. I wanted to be someone you could admire. I didn't want you seeing my weaknesses.''

Her heart went out to him, and she squeezed his fingertips to let him know. In an effort to ease his tension and make him feel less awkward about revealing his vulnerability, she grinned, rolled her eyes and replied, ''Men.''

She was happy to see him smile, but the momentary humor quickly waned.

''You see,'' he went on, ''I'd been harboring a secret

since we first married. A secret that's gnawed at my gut every day.''

Before this moment, whenever she'd discussed the old Jenny with anyone, be it Luke, or Chad, Mary, or Doc, she'd always felt detached, as if the conversation really hadn't been about her. But the apprehension exposed in her husband's eyes, his fear of being judged—by *her*—made this moment very personal, very intimate. The confession he was about to make, the secret he was ready to reveal, did have to do with his marriage to the old Jenny. But this also concerned her. The new Jenny. The woman who sat here on the mossy ground beside him.

''I rushed you into marrying me,'' he blurted. ''I didn't give you the time you needed to get over Chad. To deal with the hurt he caused you. I'm afraid you weren't completely over my brother before I elbowed my way into your affections.''

Luke stole you from me. Chad's angry accusation clanged in her head as loud as a church bell. And it looked as if Luke believed it of himself, too.

There was more to this. She could read that in her husband's sorrowful expression. And since he evidently couldn't bring himself to voice his thoughts, she did it for him.

''And my amnesia,'' she said, ''has made it impossible for you to ever find out the truth.''

He hung his head, but not before she saw that his eyes had grown moist. An ache throbbed deep in her chest. She wished so badly she could reassure him, but she couldn't. Not now. Maybe never.

Dwelling on a doubt neither one of them could do a thing about was useless. She reached up and slid her palm over his hand to get his attention.

''You know, when I first came home,'' she said, ''you

told me to focus on me and the baby. I thought I had. But I've figured out today that I've been too wrapped up in the hurt I've caused. Too preoccupied with my past behavior to even think about what I might want for my future. Or what might be best for my child.''

She glanced down at her midsection, then back up at him. ''There's no way I would be a good mother to this baby if I spend my life with a man I can't trust to be truthful. I need to be with someone I love. A man who'll love me. A man who'll make me happy.''

Praying he understood, she continued, ''I think it's more important that I provide my baby with a happy environment, than to raise him or her with the biological father.''

Luke's quiet voice held an edge as he said, ''You're talking as if you've made up your mind that Chad fathered the baby.'' His dark gaze narrowed a fraction. ''Chad's a liar. I know it. And so do you. He could be telling the whopper of his life.''

''But why?'' Utter bewilderment had her shaking her head, wrinkling her brow.

''You said it yourself,'' he pointed out. ''Ending up with you makes him the winner in the game.''

''But being saddled with a woman who doesn't love you doesn't sound like much of a victory to me.''

He shrugged. ''I'm still working it out,'' was all he would say. His eyes grew hooded. ''Those paternity tests you talked about to Chad...are they complicated things? Will taking one hurt the baby in any way?''

''No,'' she told him.

''Then I say we go for it.'' He tipped up his chin. ''I'm that confident that I fathered that child.''

Jenny thought he was doing a wonderful job of hiding all of his doubt. Almost all of it, anyway.

"I also told Chad that those tests can't prove I didn't have an affair with him," she said softly. "Can you live with the idea that your wife might have been unfaithful to you?"

With her heart pounding in her throat, she reached up and pressed her fingertips to his lips. "Don't answer that." She stood up, hoping the breezy manner in which she brushed the dirt from her clothes disguised the sudden panic that drowned her in a torrent. "Not now. We both need time to think. Besides," she told him, the lightness of her voice not quite sounding genuine, "the bugs are beginning to bite. We need to get inside."

It was a silly excuse, really. One that was meant for the sole purpose of keeping him silent. She desired this man. But she realized now that her feelings transcended the physical—she loved Luke. And she'd have offered her body to a whole hoard of stinging, biting insects if she thought for one moment Luke's response to her question was going to be anything near what she wanted to hear.

Midnight. One o'clock. One-twenty-five. Two o'clock. Jenny watched the hour hand as it made its slow, arduous trek around the face of her glow-in-the-dark alarm clock. Finally, at ten past two in the morning, she could take the tossing and turning no more.

Snapping on the light, she shoved back the covers and sat on the edge of the mattress. The night breeze fluttering the sheers was filled with the lush smells of summer. Sweet honeysuckle. The strong, acrid aroma of pine.

She reached up to rub at her left shoulder in a vain attempt to massage away the tension. Every time she closed her eyes, she saw the hurt in Luke's face when she'd asked if he could spend his life with an unfaithful wife.

That pain would take a long time to die. Her spine straightened as she realized his anguish over her unknown past might never go away.

Taking her bottom lip between her teeth, she worried it lightly. Where does this leave us? she wondered. How can we ever overcome this problem? How can either of us live with these unanswered questions?

The carpet was velvety against her bare feet as she padded to the window. Moonlight lit the mountain and trees with an ethereal halo.

She would have an easier time of it, she knew, since she had no recollection of the past. Luke was in a different boat altogether. One that didn't have a smooth course ahead of it.

A soft knock on her bedroom door made her spin around.

"Jenny?"

Her body tensed at the sound of Luke's voice.

"Are you awake?"

"Yes," she answered, hearing the anxious tremor in the single word. "Come in."

He closed the door behind him, Jenny's eyes riveted to the cotton T-shirt he wore, the jersey shorts, which did nothing to hide his taut, muscular body from view. Those heated curling tendrils of desire grew, spiraled, like tender plant roots after a feeding of rich fertilizer.

Her nipples budded to life beneath the thin satin of her nightgown. She crossed her arms over her chest to hide her body's reaction to him. She wanted this man. Had wanted him from the very beginning. But the physical attraction they felt for each other could never be strong enough to defeat the doubt and anguish over the past.

But you love him.

Yes, and the love she felt was powerful enough to conquer anything. However, it wasn't *her* emotional state that would keep them apart. Luke was the one who would be living with the unanswered questions concerning her fidelity. He was the one who must forever wrestle with the fact that his wife had once loved his brother, that at one time she'd even expected to marry him.

Her husband's hair was mussed, telling her he'd experienced the same hours and hours of restlessness she had. His eyes held a haunted look that made her want to tell him to go away. To leave her be. That she couldn't bear to hear his rejection.

She wanted to shout, to yell, to stomp her feet, wave her arms. But nothing was going to stop the renunciation she was certain he was about to impart. And she couldn't even bring herself to be angry. Because she understood. She understood all he was feeling. The fear. The doubt. The anxiety of the unknown. Because she'd felt all those things herself. *About* herself.

"I've been sitting on the steps," he told her. "I couldn't sleep. Then I saw your light come on."

She nodded, and the night silence settled over the room.

Then he said, "I don't want you to have a paternity test done." The sentence seemed to burst from him like an intense explosion of fireworks.

Jenny blinked, uncertain that she'd heard him correctly. The paternity test was the last thing she'd expected to hear him talk about.

"I don't care who fathered the baby," he said. "All I care about is that—" he paused "—I'm his daddy. And that you and I raise him together." He paused long enough to swallow tightly. "I love you, Jenny. And I can't even think about life without you."

Was he really standing there? she wondered. Saying

these marvelous things? Or could this be some kind of wishful fantasy she would soon awaken from?

She clasped her hands together in front of her, afraid to speak, afraid to move.

"You asked me earlier if I could live with the idea that you might have turned to Chad," he said. "You were a wonderful wife. Loving, caring, giving. I think if we were to find out that you had been unfaithful, you would be just as hurt, just as upset by the news as I." He inhaled a jerky, emotional breath. "I was wrong not to have talked to you about my stupid fears. I was wrong to separate myself from you. I shouldn't have let my doubts come between us. Can you ever forgive me, sweetheart? Can you let me love you? Can you let me love our baby?"

Before she could answer, he said, "I want be the one who's there when he takes his first step. I want to pitch him his first baseball. I want to buy him his first fire truck."

Her heart soared. He loved her. He wanted her. He wanted to raised her child as theirs.

The treble of her voice wavered as she asked, "How can you be so sure we're going to have a son?"

Her use of the plural pronoun wasn't lost on him, and he was across the room in a flash, his arms enveloping her in a strong, warm and secure embrace.

The heat of his mouth on her neck was scorching.

"If we have a daughter, I'll attend her first tea party," he whispered against her ear. "I'll buy her first doll." He nibbled her earlobe.

The smile that spread across her mouth was one of pure, erotic joy, and she couldn't wait to reciprocate with a little nibbling of her own—but not until she teased him a bit more first.

"What if she wants a fire truck?" she murmured.

A gentle rumble erupted from deep in his chest in answer, and he reached down, picked her up and carried her to the bed.

"Then I'll buy her a fire truck *and* a doll," he whispered, laying her down on the mattress and pressing his body against the length of her. His lips blazed a trail down her jaw as his palm captured her breast, his skin sliding against the satiny fabric of her nightgown.

The hard heat of his desire nudged her thigh and her breath quickened in her throat. His name passed her lips in a raw and hungry whisper. Her eyes flew open at the sound of his groan and she reveled in, writhed in, the passion filling his black-as-midnight eyes.

His kiss was long, deep and possessive.

She slid the arch of her foot along the taut muscle of his calf, shifting her hips in an unspoken invitation. He accepted her passionate summons, his knee rising slowing, urging her legs to part. His hand felt lava-hot as he smoothed it down the length of her torso, over the small swell of her tummy, finally cupping the blazing fire of her femininity.

Sparks flashed behind her closed eyelids as a stab of lightning-quick pain knifed across her brain. She gasped in reaction, but the agony had already faded. Images whizzed in her head at the speed of light. Pictures from every stage of her life, like trillions of stars in space, flew past at a frightening speed.

In the time it took an eye to blink, a heart to beat, she remembered all the experiences of her life. Joy, pain, loneliness, success, failure, determination, fear, hate, love. Every single experience was there. Every single one.

The memory at the forefront of her mind was the one that had been made at Simon's Point. The place of her accident. The deserted and dangerous place she'd been lured to.

The kiss she felt was not Luke's, but Chad's. The grabbing, hurtful hands she felt on her body were not Luke's, but Chad's. She opened her eyes wide, murmuring a confused and panic-stricken protest, and the eyes staring back at her were not Luke's, but Chad's.

"No!" The denial was torn from her throat in a strangled scream. She punched and slapped, kicked and shoved, until she was free of his weight, free of his touch.

He called her name, but she was frantic to flee. Run! Escape!

Caught up in the harrowing memory, she felt hands on her back, and then she was falling, rolling, tumbling down the rocky incline of the Point.

"Luke!" she cried, her eyes streaming sight-blurring tears. Her last thought before unconsciousness overtook her, she remembered now, had been that of her beloved husband.

"I'm here," Luke said, wrapping her in his arms. "I'm here."

She heard her husband's voice. She was not at the Point. Her knees weak and shaky, she blinked, realizing that she was standing by the door of her bedroom, wrapped in Luke's embrace. A moment ago, all she'd seen was bare rock and slippery shale, but now she saw the solid wood of the bedroom door under her hand, felt the soft carpet under her feet. And Luke's strong, protective hands around her waist.

"Oh, God," she whispered, icy perspiration prickling her skin.

"What, honey?" Deep concern, fear and confusion were all evident in his raw tone. "What is it?"

"I remember." A violent tremor shook her body. "I remember it all."

Hours later, they sat curled on the bed, his whole body a warm shield against the horrible memory of that day. Against the memory of the awful weeks preceding that day. They'd talked everything out. More than once. Still, Luke patiently listened as her need to vent resurfaced one more time.

"I really don't think he pushed me," she said. "I don't think Chad meant for me to be hurt."

"He only meant to frighten you." Suppressed anger laced the edges of Luke's sarcastic words. "To intimidate you."

"Well—" her tone was barely a whisper "—that *was* his way." It wasn't an excuse for Chad's behavior, she was simply stating fact. "It had been, ever since I first met him. Back in college, I mean. I was so naive. So ignorant of the opposite sex. I thought his behavior was…manly. Masculine. I thought that's how it was between men and women."

Luke's torso stiffened at this new piece of information. "He forced himself on you…?"

"No," she quickly assured him. "Nothing like that. Not while we dated in college, anyway." She took a long moment to inhale. "Our relationship was complicated." Then she let out a disgusted sigh. "Who am I kidding? I was a fool. Chad pretty much ordered me around the whole time we dated. He threatened me with other girls. Even went out on me a few times. Just like you told me."

She twisted in Luke's arms, placed the flat of her hand on his now naked chest. "You have to realize, I had no idea what love was. All I knew was the shallow game he played. Heck, it was a game all my college friends played." She shook her head. "I mean, my own room-mate wanted to date Chad, and she thought it was okay to go after him." Her voice dropped to an embarrassed whisper when she added, "Chad took her up on her offer, too. It was a humiliating experience. But he always came back to me."

Luke was silent and Jenny felt her face flame with hot shame as she contemplated her own words. "I was an idiot, wasn't I? An awful idiot. But it was only because I didn't realize that the love Chad offered me was so su-perficial, so full of conditions." She gazed up at him through lowered lashes. "I didn't learn what true love really was until you showed me."

Luke's taut muscles relaxed, and he pulled her close. She pressed her cheek to his chest.

"You proved to me just how caring and giving love was supposed to be," she told him. "You showed me that making love should be a wondrous experience of give and take. Something beautiful between a man and woman. Not the intimidating encounter Chad always made it. There was always the threat that if I didn't put out, there was some girl waiting outside the bedroom door who would be more than willing to satisfy him. And afterwards, I felt as if he strutted around like a bandy rooster who had just claimed ownership. Sex with Chad was dreadful. Dread-ful."

Lifting her chin, she said, "I'm sorry, Luke. You shouldn't have to be hearing this. But I'm grateful that you're listening to me."

"It's okay," he assured her.

His chuckle vibrated in his chest, the sound of it deep and rich to her ear, pressed against his pectoral muscle.

"I might not be so calm and secure," he said, "if I had to hear about you and Chad having great sex."

Even though Luke joked about being her sounding board, Jenny knew it took a confident and self-assured man to listen to his wife's sexual past, especially when that past involved his own brother. Well, she was pleased to realize one thing. Once all this was out in the open, there would never be a need to hurt him with it again. The past would be behind them.

But in order for that to happen, she'd have to get everything out in the open. Everything.

"Luke?"

"Hmmm?"

She steeled herself with an inhalation. "I told you that I fought Chad off at the Point. That I was running away from him when I fell..."

He grew utterly still as he waited for her to continue.

"I'm sure, though, that he had every intention of—" she hesitated "—that he meant to—" She stopped, swallowed.

"Rape you," he finished when it became apparent she simply couldn't say the word.

"Yes," she whispered. "I really believe he had some twisted notion that if he could get me to have sex with him that I'd become his, or something. He had been pushing me and pushing me to have an affair with him for weeks before he lured me to Simon's Point." She tucked a strand of hair behind her ear. "He told me you had some news for me about our plans to build a house, and that you wanted me to meet you there. It never entered my head that he might be lying."

They were quiet for some time.

"You aren't the only one he pushed," Luke told her. "He argued with me for weeks to sign over half the resort to him. He used everything he could think of, even throwing Dad's dream in my face, in an effort to make me do his bidding. I wanted to work the resort with him. I wanted to try and make Dad's dream a reality. But I felt I needed to see Chad prove himself. I needed to see some sign that Prentice Mountain meant more to him than a simple piece of real estate that would be very easy to sell. I couldn't sign over even a small percentage of ownership, not when so many people rely on the resort for their living.''

After a moment, Jenny said, ''So that's what Doc meant.''

''Doc?''

She nodded. ''Yes, Doc said that everyone remotely connected to the resort has been nervous since Chad's return. He must have meant that the employees are afraid of how Chad might affect the business if you took him on as partner.''

''The folks in Olem don't have to worry.'' Luke's whole body grew rigid with anger. ''My brother's the one who should worry. I've figured out his plan. He couldn't get to me, so he went after you. Hard and relentlessly, it seems.''

Jenny could only nod in agreement. ''I still don't understand what he thought he'd get out of pursuing me.''

''Half the resort, of course. If he could get you to leave me,'' Luke said, ''and marry him, he'd get his hands on your divorce settlement.''

''That's pretty far-fetched, don't you think?''

''For any normal hardworking person, yes, but have you ever known Chad to do much thinking?'' Then Luke added, ''Chad has always been so self-centered, I guess he just couldn't see his plan not working out.''

Jenny was relieved to know that Luke saw his brother clearly. She felt her husband had spent too many years beating himself up for not liking Chad, when all along Chad had never been a very likable person.

"Why would he risk claiming your baby as his when he had to know I'd tell you that I hadn't slept with him?"

"Ah, but Chad didn't claim the baby until after it was clear that you were suffering with amnesia from your head injury." Luke's laugh was humorless. "On the other hand, I guess my baby brother does think. Otherwise, he wouldn't have schemed to take advantage of the situation."

She sighed, but then her voice firmed as she said, "I can't stay on Prentice Mountain. Not if he's going to be here."

"Don't worry," Luke told her. "He's leaving. Tomorrow."

She was so surprised that she sat up and stared at him. "What about your promise to your father? What about the promise you made to Chad to always have a job for him? What about your dad's dream of you and Chad working together..." Her voice caught and Luke's eyes widened as he evidently realized *her* secret.

"The Prentice way," he said. "I rammed it down your throat so much that you felt you couldn't come to me when Chad began to pressure you with his advances. Isn't that right?"

It took her a moment to answer. "I knew it was important to you for Chad to be here. I knew how much you wanted to fulfil your father's dream."

"Can you ever forgive me for putting you through all that?"

She shook her head, her fingers sliding across his skin. "There's nothing to forgive. I love you."

"And I love you," he told her. "More than words can

say." He searched her face for a moment. "Looks like it's high time for me to live my own dreams."

Her brows raised as she wondered what he meant.

"My father had his whole lifetime to dream his dreams," he went on. "To bring them to fruition. But it turned out that there were too many forces working against him. However, I can't take responsibility for that.

"Chad had his dream, too. He toured Europe. He burned up every cent of his inheritance doing it. I can't take responsibility for that, either.

"I have to conjure up my own dreams, don't I? It's just not natural for a person to be try to fulfil someone else's dream. I have to live my own. And my dream is building the resort to the best it's ever been. My dream is being here. With you. With our child."

Jenny had assured him hours ago that there was no chance that this baby was any man's but his, that it had been their love that conceived the child she carried. She knew that information was what allowed him to listen and talk so calmly about everything that had occurred between himself and his brother.

"I have a dream, too," she said.

He smiled. "Tell me."

"I want us to have the perfect marriage."

His mouth quirked into a grin. "That's a pretty tall order."

"I don't mean I want a relationship where we never argue," she said. "That'd be foolish, especially when I like making up so much. But I do want us to be able to talk. About anything. I want you to be able to come to me with any troubles you might have. And I don't ever want you to move out of our bedroom again. For any reason."

"Agreed." He pulled her close. "And I want you to

come to me if some man makes you feel uncomfortable, or threatened.''

"Oh," she said, "once Chad is gone, that's not going to happen.''

"You never know," he told her. "You're a beautiful woman.''

She snuggled against his chest, kind of liking the idea that he found her so attractive he was sure other men would do the same.

"I feel good," she told him. "I feel sure we would have been together in the end. Even if I hadn't remembered my past.''

"Of course we would have," he told her, his fingers combing through her hair. "Don't you know that true love always wins out?''

She smiled, his chest hairs tickling her nose. Then she asked, "But why do you think I remembered now? Tonight? Why would my amnesia clear so suddenly?''

She sensed him shake his head.

"Who knows how the brain works?" he said. "The most logical explanation I can come up with is that your subconscious was giving you the chance to look at your situation from a fresh point of view.''

"What do you mean?''

He lifted one shoulder. "Well, you disagreed with my reasons for allowing Chad to be here, yet the old Jenny couldn't bring herself to point that out to me. But because of your amnesia, you were able to ask me why I continued to suffer Chad's presence.''

She remembered the day she'd confronted him about living in the house with someone he so obviously didn't like and didn't get along with.

"You made me question myself about living my father's dream rather than my own," he went on. "Maybe your subconscious realized you could only do that if you were free of the past, free to think about and see things in a new way, free to be more assertive.''

After planting a hot, luscious kiss on his chest, she gazed up into his face as she ran her fingertips over his nipple, smiling inwardly when she felt it tighten under her touch. ''That is one thing about me that *has* changed for the better, don't you think?''

His gaze darkened with desire, and other—lower— parts of his body responded to her, too.

''Ah, yes,'' he whispered. ''I do love your newfound assertiveness.''

Epilogue

The green branches of the pines drooped low with a heavy layer of snow. Sunshine glinted off the pristine whiteness. In the distance, Jenny heard the faint calls and laughter of height-of-the-season skiers on the mountain slopes. She sighed contentedly as she took a moment to survey the wintry scene.

"Nose for no-man?"

The high-pitched voice had her grinning and she looked down at her beautiful, two-year-old, snowsuited son.

"You think our snowman needs a nose, huh?" she said. Pulling a perfect orange carrot from her pocket, Jenny offered it to him. "Will this do, sir?"

The child squealed with glee, running at her and shouting a gleeful, "Fanks, Mommy," as he took the carrot. He stood up on tiptoe, but still could not reach the snowman's face. "Help," he called.

Jenny laughed. Swooping him up high, she reveled in his carefree laughter. Then she lifted him toward the fat snowman. "Give him his nose, Daniel," she said.

"Daddy will be home for lunch soon and we want Mr. Snowman to be perfect."

Daniel pushed the carrot into the topmost snowball, right where its left cheekbone should have been located, but Jenny shouted out praise just the same.

"No-man!" Daniel yelled happily and clapped his approval of the finished product.

"He looks great," Jenny said. "And now we're ready for Daddy." Her voice lowered conspiratorially. "After lunch we can tell him our secret."

"See-kit." Daniel's eyes grew round as he worked his tongue around the difficult syllables.

Jenny nodded. Just then a lightly packed snowball struck her square in the back, making her gasp as splattering snow found its way beneath the collar of her coat. She turned and saw her handsome husband standing in the drive, his gorgeous black eyes virtuously averted as he whistled a few random notes over and over.

"You look about as innocent as the devil himself." She set Daniel on his feet and scooped up a handful of snow, packing it tight.

Her son giggled. "No-ball! No-ball!" he said, reaching toward her.

She handed him the icy ball and then scooped up another handful of snow.

"Let's get Daddy," she whispered, but then she saw Luke rushing at her, an arsenal of snowy ammunition in his hands.

Her hoot was full of fun as she ran from him. "Don't you dare," she laughingly shouted over her shoulder. But it was too late. The impact on her shoulder sent snow straight into her face. He then tackled her, and they rolled together on the cold blanket of white.

Luke kissed her chilled, wet lips, his mouth warm on her icy skin. Daniel was still laughing as he reached them.

"Get Daddy," Jenny urged. "Throw the snowball at Daddy."

The child tossed the snowball, and it landed right on Jenny's chin. Luke's eyes glinted with humor as he chuckled at the irony.

"Never try to turn a son against his father," he said.

She simply laughed as she sputtered and swiped at the snow in her face.

"Okay—" his face loomed close "—what's this secret you and Daniel were talking about?"

"Secret?" She used a tone meant to convey she had no idea what he was talking about.

"See-kit," Daniel parroted, and Jenny had to grin at the wonder in his huge, black eyes.

Tugging on the sleeve of his son's snowsuit, Luke said, "Tell Daddy, Daniel."

The boy looked at Jenny and she nodded silent permission.

"Me no baby," he said importantly. "Doc sez."

Luke frowned. He looked at Jenny. "I know you had a checkup today," he told her. "But I didn't know Doc was going to have a look at Daniel."

"He didn't."

Bewilderment knit Luke's brow. "Then what—"

"Patience," Jenny said. "Daniel, what else did Doc say?"

Daniel pointed to his chest and, in a boastful voice, said, "Me big bro-ver."

All was silent for a moment or two while Luke processed this information. Finally, he grinned at Daniel. "Well, way to go, little buddy." Then he looked at his wife. "You mean it?"

She nodded, gazing lovingly at him. "Doc confirmed it today."

"Lord," he told her, "I couldn't be happier."

Jenny studied his face, a worried crease marring her forehead. "Are you sure?"

From some unexplainable psychic connection, he seemed to know exactly what was troubling her.

"Absolutely." He ran his fingers lightly down her jaw. "Don't give my brother another thought."

"But a man should have his family nearby," she said.

"I have my family nearby." He smiled gently. "You're here with me. And Daniel. And now there's another one on the way." One shoulder hitched up with the briefest of shrugs. "Besides, Chad's doing great as a ski instructor in Aspen. He's surviving on his own. That's how it should be."

His grin was so delectable she thought for sure she could just eat him right up.

"I'm more than happy," he assured her. "How could I not be when I'm living every single dream I've ever had?"

Without giving her time to answer, he tucked his face in the curve of her neck and rolled them down the snowy bank, their son squealing gleefully close behind.

* * * * *

Donna Clayton's MOTHER & CHILD series will continue soon from Silhouette Romance.

HERE COME THE
Virgin Brides!

Celebrate the joys of first love with more unforgettable stories from Romance's brightest stars:

SWEET BRIDE OF REVENGE
by Suzanne Carey—June 1998 (SR #1300)

Reader favorite Suzanne Carey weaves a sensuously powerful tale about a man who forces the daughter of his enemy to be his bride of revenge. But what happens when this hard-hearted husband falls head over heels...for his wife?

THE BOUNTY HUNTER'S BRIDE
by Sandra Steffen—July 1998 (SR #1306)

In this provocative page-turner by beloved author Sandra Steffen, a shotgun wedding is only the beginning when an injured bounty hunter and the sweet seductress who'd nursed him to health are discovered in a remote mountain cabin by her gun-toting dad and *four* brothers!

SUDDENLY...MARRIAGE!
by Marie Ferrarella—August 1998 (SR #1312)

RITA Award-winning author Marie Ferrarella weaves a magical story set in sultry New Orleans about two people determined to remain single who exchange vows in a mock ceremony during Mardi Gras, only to learn their bogus marriage is the real thing....

And look for more VIRGIN BRIDES in future months, only in—

❤ *Silhouette* ROMANCE™

Available at your favorite retail outlet.

Look us up on-line at: http://www.romance.net   SRVBJ-A

In **July 1998** comes

THE
MACKENZIE
FAMILY

by *New York Times* bestselling author

LINDA
HOWARD

The dynasty continues with:

Mackenzie's Pleasure: Rescuing a pampered ambassador's daughter from her terrorist kidnappers was a piece of cake for navy SEAL Zane Mackenzie. It was only afterward, when they were alone together, that the real danger began....

Mackenzie's Magic: Talented trainer Maris Mackenzie was wanted for horse theft, but with no memory, she had little chance of proving her innocence or eluding the real villains. Her only hope for salvation? The stranger in her bed.

Available this July for the first time ever in a two-in-one trade-size edition. Fall in love with the Mackenzies for the first time—or all over again!

Available at your favorite retail outlet.

Silhouette Books